SHOTGUNNING

SHOTGUNNING

Michael Clark

PANTAXIS PRESS

Copyright © Michael Clark 2011
First published in 2011 by Pantaxis Press
26 Montpelier Street, Brighton, BN1 3DL

Distributed by Gardners Books, 1 Whittle Drive, Eastbourne,
East Sussex, BN23 6QH
Tel: +44(0)1323 521555 | Fax: +44(0)1323 521666

www. pantaxispress.co.uk

The right of Michael Clark to be identified as the author of the work has been asserted herein in accordance with the Copyright, Designs and Patents Act 1988.

All rights reserved. This book is sold subject to the condition that it shall not, by way of trade or otherwise, be lent, resold, hired out or otherwise circulated without the publisher's prior consent in any form of binding or cover other than that in which it is published and without a similar condition including this condition being imposed on the subsequent purchaser.

All the characters in this book are fictitious and any resemblance to actual people, living or dead, is purely imaginary.

British Library Cataloguing in Publication Data
A catalogue record for this book is available from
the British Library.

ISBN 978-09566219-0-0

Typeset by Amolibros, Milverton, Somerset
www.amolibros.co.uk
This book production has been managed by Amolibros
Printed and bound by T J International Ltd, Padstow, Cornwall, UK

For Paul

Shotgunning is a...trick used by pseudo-psychics and false mediums. To convince one's mark that one is truly in touch with the other world, one provides a large quantity of information, some of which is bound to seem appropriate.

The Skeptic's Dictionary
Robert Todd Carroll

Calumet,

April, 1998

Imagine this. On Friday you spent the best part of three hours watching a video of a film that was on television a week ago. It was a Western called Shotgunning, and it starred Harold Masters as Gabriel Jones, an evangelical preacher with paranormal powers.

You've heard a lot about Masters, but nothing to prepare you for the letter you found on your doorstep this morning. It's from him – Harold Masters – and in it he claims to possess the same powers as the man he portrayed in the film. For instance, he says, he can listen in to conversations at any distance.

What do you think? Do you think he's lying? Perhaps you think he's mad? Or do you think instead of a recent conversation of your own, and hope to God he didn't overhear that?

Imagine this, the letter starts...

I do possess the same powers as Gabriel Jones, and I can listen in to conversations at any distance. I was doing it last Friday evening, lying here in my caravan at Calumet, while a hundred miles away in Denby Green, Tim was thanking Nora Johnson for opening up shop after hours to sell him some aspirin.

"I think I must be going mad," he said, when Nora handed him his change. "I could have sworn I saw some in the bathroom cabinet this afternoon, but Heather reckons we ran out days ago."

If only I'd followed up on that.

But no, because it isn't just the spoken word I can listen in to. I can read minds as well, and one look into Mrs Johnson's eyes was enough to tell me she wasn't really taking in what Tim was saying. She was too keen to get the supper dishes out of the way in time for the film, which was due to start on Channel Four in twenty minutes. It was a Western called *Shotgunning*, and according to the local paper, it starred Harold Masters as Gabriel Jones, an evangelical preacher with paranormal powers. Imagine that.

Strangely enough, my unusual gifts came about as a result of a knock on the head I received during the filming of *Shotgunning*, an event that coincided with the exact moment of Tim's entrance into the world. I know, because I saw it as clearly as if I'd been present at the birth, instead of several thousand miles away in a mocked-up Western saloon. When I came to, I managed to persuade myself I must have been dreaming – until the telegram arrived – and I was on my way to Tim's christening when I discovered this place.

I never did tell Tim about my powers — in fact the weight of responsibility that came with them was so enormous, I was always a bit cautious about using them at all — but I did suspect I was capable of much more than listening in to conversations and reading minds. So the day after Tim drowned I decided to try something.

I was sitting under my favourite tree in the top field here at Calumet. It's a horse chestnut, and when Tim used to visit me as a boy we would often walk by and admire it. In autumn we'd stop and look for conkers, but someone had always beaten us to it, and all the husks on the ground round about would be empty. If we did manage to find a stick heavy enough to throw with any accuracy, it would usually manage to lodge itself in a branch somewhere just out of reach, and as often as not we would come away empty-handed.

The tree was bare last Saturday, but sitting on the ground with my back against its trunk, I managed to conjure up an image of a ripe nut hanging from the branch above me. I willed it to be there, and before long — miraculously — I knew it was. I didn't need to look. I just held out my hand, and down it fell into my open palm, splitting open as it did to reveal the biggest, shiniest conker I have ever seen. Tim would have loved it.

'Vengeance is mine; I will repay, saith the Lord.'

Tim's father quoted that at me once, when I as good as called him a coward for backing away from a fight. I'll never forget it. A couple of yobs had cornered him in an alley, and helped themselves to his wallet. When he told me, I was all for going after them to teach them a lesson. But Oliver had more sense, and I was let off the hook by a line from the Bible.

It's a different story now, of course, but then, as Oliver also used to say, God does move in a mysterious way...

And that was where it ended, this first draft of Harold's letter, which he kept in a trunk full of fan mail and newspaper cuttings…a box of old photographs…a bundle of personal correspondence…and a carrier bag containing a pair of grey pinstriped trousers, a white cotton shirt, a black string tie, a bowler hat and an embroidered silk waistcoat, gold on gold.

Friday, 17

September 1968

Missing star found in Kent

It was revealed last night that Hollywood legend, Harold Masters, who had not been seen since attending a christening in Norfolk last Tuesday morning, is alive and safe, and staying in a farmhouse somewhere near Tunbridge Wells, where he is recovering from an injury sustained on the set of his latest epic, *Shotgunning*.

Doctors in Los Angeles had advised him not to travel, after he was mildly concussed by a piece of falling scenery two weeks ago, but...

Harold never talked about his love life – past or present – so most of what Cassie knew about it came from old film magazines and newspaper features. The rest she had worked out for herself, so when she saw his caravan rocking up and down on the plot next to hers, she pictured him making love to Esther Savage, not as they were now, but as they had been in the autumn of 1968, when Esther visited The Foundation for the first time. The Calumet

Foundation, that is, where Harold had been living for nearly thirty years now, but even at that distance, Cassie could still see the look of delight on his face when he opened his door to find Esther standing there.

She'd been Esther Court then – fifteen years married to Oliver Court, and with a two-month old baby in tow – but that hadn't fooled Cassie for one minute. And nor had it escaped her notice that every time Esther had visited since, she'd brought young Timothy with her. But not Oliver. Never Oliver.

Nearly thirty years on, and Tim was married himself now – to a television celebrity called Heather Swallows, who had yet to honour The Foundation with a visit – but Tim still came when he could – every inch his mother's son – and was following in Harold's footsteps as one of the most popular actors of his generation.

Esther, on the other hand, had stopped coming a few years ago, when Oliver became too ill to be left alone; and Cassie's hopes of a happy ending had suffered a further setback in January, when Esther married another man less than a year after Oliver died. David Savage…

But it was going to take more than one or two inconvenient facts to cure Cassie of the idea that it was into Harold's arms that Esther would fall when the final credits began to roll.

Cassie had known Harold since the day he moved to Calumet, at a time when the community's principal objective was to promote love and peace through spiritual awakening. It wasn't so widely known then, although it did get the occasional mention in articles and documentaries about cranky religious sects. In fact it was nothing of the sort. It didn't recruit as such – you would never find a pair of handsome Calumetians grinning on your doorstep for instance, or attempting to befriend the homesick fresher on campus – and it was as easy to leave as it was to join. But not for Cassie. She had lived here all her life.

Her parents had come over from California in the early fifties, and brought with them the idea of running courses on arts and crafts to generate income. It had taken years to catch on, but by the time they went back in the mid-seventies, The Foundation had become a slick commercial enterprise with a brochure advertising workshops on every New Age phenomenon from Astral Projection to Tantric Sex.

Cassie's speciality was quilt making, and her workshops on the subject were always quick to sell out. That was the reason she invariably gave for having decided to stay on when her parents left. And she lived in the caravan next door to Harold's.

She was on her way there now, to watch her favourite film on television. But first there was the matter of a rocking Wagonmaster to look into. What was Harold doing in there?

It was definitely him. She could hear his groans quite clearly now, and the creak of the wooden slats under his mattress, as he thrashed around on his bunk. But she didn't really believe he had anyone in there with him. Apart from anything else his curtains were open.

Half a minute later the upturned recycling box that doubled as Cassie's front door step was in position under Harold's window, and she was just about to climb on to it, when she asked herself again: what might he be doing in there? Because if he was on his own, and she did look in, that might turn out to be even more embarrassing than if he had company. On the other hand she couldn't just leave it. He might be having a fit. Perhaps she should knock? Or would it be better to call out, and ask him if he was all right? Trouble was, if she did that, and there really was someone in there with him…

A moment later she had one foot back on the box, ready to climb up and peep in, when the thrashing suddenly stopped, the caravan rocked to a halt, and, after an agonising silence which froze her to the spot, she heard Harold's voice call out:

"Not now, Cassie, if you don't mind. I was just having a bad dream, that's all."

"But…?"

"Please, Cass. I'll be all right. We'll talk in the morning."

'I was like a rabbit caught in a car's headlights,' she would write in her diary the following day. *'And Harold was the driver who stopped just in time.'*

Right now, though, she could hear her bedside alarm ringing. The film was about to begin.

It was a Western called *Shotgunning*, and it starred Harold as Gabriel Jones, an evangelical preacher with paranormal powers, who sold patent medicines from the step of a covered waggon by day, and wreaked his own peculiar brand of vengeance on unrepentant sinners by night.

A fall downstairs, a suicide, an accidental overdose – three apparently unconnected deaths – but Cassie knew better, because she'd seen the film before, and it turned out that Gabriel was responsible for bringing them all about…by will alone. A load of nonsense, of course, but Harold's performance was so convincing, Cassie invariably found herself playing along.

Cassie had all Harold's films on video, but there was something special about watching them when they were being broadcast 'live' on television. All those millions of other people watching at the same time. It made her feel connected.

Heather…

Heather Swallows was standing shoulder deep in the shallow end of the Manor House swimming pool, holding her husband's head clear of the water, while she waited for the emergency services to arrive. Police and ambulance, she imagined, although she hadn't waited for the operator to put her through – just blurted out something about Tim drowning, before abandoning the phone and jumping back into the pool. A taxi driver had told her recently that you didn't need to give your name and address any more. It automatically came up on the screen when your call was connected. But she had had the presence of mind to unlock the patio doors and switch on the lights before dialling 999. So she knew they'd have no trouble finding her.

She'd met Tim at a party in Little Venice three years ago, when he was working with the RSC, and she was a competitive swimmer who had never quite made it into the national squad.

When he spotted her, she was talking to her brother, Gerry, about fame and its rewards, and the lengths each of them would be prepared to go to get what they wanted. What Heather wanted most was financial security, and having reached this stage of her career without attracting a serious sponsor, she was beginning to realise a change in tactics was called for. But there were limits…

She said as much to Gerry, and a moment later Tim walked up and introduced himself. Six weeks later they were married.

When Heather was approached by Tim's agent shortly after she got back from her honeymoon, she knew it had nothing to do with her prowess in the swimming pool, but she was so eager to get on, it didn't cross her mind to ask him how he was intending to market her. Her first scheduled television appearance was as a contestant on a celebrity quiz, and it hardly mattered at all when the host introduced her as Mrs Timothy Court. But it did matter when he was still doing it six months later, and it mattered even more that Tim was so understanding when she complained to him about it. He'd have done better to laugh in her face – like her brother would have. Because that was the trouble. Over the years, Heather had developed a taste for men like Gerry – men who put themselves first, and thought feminism was for lesbians. Tim was too politically correct for her, and it wasn't long before she realised how much happier she'd be without him.

Leaving him was not an option – not while her success was as Mrs Timothy Court, anyway – and besides, for the most part she liked things as they were – the apartment in London, the Manor House in Denby Green. Tim had even bought Gerry a little cottage down the lane. It was just the man himself.

There was always the possibility he might die, of course, and she was soon weighing up the chances…of a heart attack, say, or a fatal stroke, although neither seemed likely with Tim's healthy lifestyle. She quickly ruled out cancer, and everything else that might involve a lingering death, and turned her mind to less natural causes.

A car crash, perhaps, or a plane crash or a train crash – he did travel a lot. On the other hand, it was a well-known fact that most accidents happened in the home. An electric shock then…or a fall…or…?

Heather often found herself daydreaming about how she would react to the news, and invariably came out in favour of putting on a brave face. It was what Tim would want, she decided, and the hypothetical phone call to her late husband's mother always brought tears to her eyes…until she came to her senses.

Now, though, at last, her dreams had come true. Or at least one of them had. Because tonight, just a few days after his third wedding anniversary, Tim had drowned – in the Manor House swimming pool – and the emergency services would be arriving any minute.

Esther…

Esther Savage was watching *Shotgunning*, her labrador, Ben, curled up on Dave's chair beside her. Dave didn't like Ben climbing on the furniture, but then Dave never came home much before two on a Saturday morning, Friday night being lock-in night at the Regent for him and a few of his cronies. So Esther let Ben do just what he liked.

She'd met Dave when she put the Hampstead house

up for sale last September. Viewing was supposed to be by appointment only, but he'd knocked on the off chance, and his success had been in making her laugh. Her first husband, Oliver, had died the previous year, and there hadn't been much to laugh at before or since. In fact she hadn't even realised there was a frivolous side to her nature – until Dave came along.

She was showing him around the kitchen when he asked her out for lunch, and she could hardly believe the cheek of the man, particularly when he said he knew a nice little place in Brighton. But it turned out he lived there, and it was only lunch after all. So she went.

The restaurant was crowded, and Dave seemed to know everyone there, including the staff, who all called him by his first name and treated him like a friend. When Esther chose the chef's special, the waiter pulled a face, and recommended something else, so she took his advice, and enjoyed it all the more for having been tipped the wink. In all her sixty-seven years, nothing like that had ever happened to her. And the noise! Oliver would have hated it!

In the taxi on the way back to the station, Dave said how much he'd enjoyed himself, and Esther was disappointed when he didn't ask to see her again. But it was hardly surprising – he must have been at least ten years her junior – so she didn't push her luck, and on the train home she almost managed to persuade herself it was for the best.

A couple of weeks later he showed up on her doorstep again, this time with another man, who he introduced as his old racing buddy, Roger. They'd bumped into each other in the casino the night before, and when Roger had mentioned he was looking for a place in town, Dave had immediately made the connection.

So it was business that had brought him back, and Esther couldn't help feeling another little tug of disappointment, but she wasn't going to let it show, and it just so happened that the house was still on the market. She'd accepted an offer on it a fortnight ago – the day after she'd had lunch with Dave, in fact – but the estate agent had phoned yesterday to say the deal had fallen through. So Roger was in luck.

His offer was a few thousand short of what Esther was asking, but on the other hand she could save almost that much on agent's fees if she took the house off the market, and did the deal privately. That was what Dave suggested anyway, and he seemed to know what he was talking about. He would help her if she liked…?

The film was just about to start again, after yet another commercial break, when Esther noticed Ben looking up at her hopefully. It must be time for his biscuits. But before she could get up and fetch them, the television screen went blank, and a voice said:

"Before we return to tonight's sixties' classic, we are going over to Gillian Green in the newsroom."

There is something compelling about a newsflash.

"Timothy Court, the actor has been found dead at his Wiltshire home."

Victor…

Another busy night at Alfredo's Trattoria. Just a few weeks ago, this seedy corner of town would have been deserted at such a late hour, but recently Alfredo's had dusted itself off, and started enjoying the patronage of some of London's most fashionable people. Soon they would move on, and before long their disciples would move on too. Then the dust would settle on Alfredo's floor once more. But for the moment, it was the place to be.

There were only two waiters left on duty now, the last main course having gone out more than an hour ago, and they were standing at the bar, waiting to order drinks from the barman, who had disappeared into the stillroom for a smoke. One of them nodded towards the foursome at the table in the window.

"See that bloke on five?" he said. "The one with his back to us? I had an unfortunate experience with him the other night."

"Did you?" said the other. "What sort of experience?"

"I caught him giving me a blow job."

"You what?"

"Yeh, straight up…if you'll pardon the expression. In the darkroom at the Bear and Whippet. I was just beginning to think my luck had changed, when the guy next to me struck a match, and there he was…right up to his epiglottis on my knob-end."

A muffled shriek, and then the second waiter said:

"You do know who he is, don't you?"

"No, who?"

"Victor Andrews."

"Never heard of him."

"Yes you have. Victor Andrews…the agent…known to his friends as Julie, apparently, on account of this film she was in…"

"Who was…?"

"Julie Andrews."

"Oh, I see…"

"Yeh, it was about this guy called Victor, you see, only he turned out to be a transvestite called Victoria or something."

"And Julie Andrews was in it?"

"Mmm…"

"That's funny. It doesn't sound like her sort of thing at all, does it?"

"No, I don't suppose it does, now that you come to mention it. Anyway, never mind that. What did you do?"

"About what…? Oh, you mean when I found myself being eaten alive by Mary Poppins over there?"

Another muffled shriek.

"Um, let me think now, what did I do? Oh, yes, I know. I said: 'Oh, look! Isn't that Dick Van Dyke over in the corner…?' and while she was distracted, I scarpered."

Victor, Alan, Simon, Ronnie…

Victor Andrews was just about to order another round of drinks when he was disturbed by a scream of laughter from behind him somewhere. Victor was one of that rare breed of actors' agents who are more famous than most of their clients, so he was used to being the centre of attention, but he would not have liked the idea of being laughed at on any terms but his own, so it was probably just as well he had his back to the bar.

In his mid-fifties now, Victor's success had come late, when two-and-a-half years ago Timothy Court had raised a few eyebrows by abandoning Delaney and Delaney, a long-established and highly reputable theatrical agency, to throw in his lot with an agency very few people had even heard of. Where Timothy had led, scores of others had followed, and suddenly, it seemed, Victor Andrews could do no wrong.

Victor had a taste for young men – the prettier the better – and the pretty young man by his side this evening filled the bill nicely – for the time being. Alan was his name, and Victor had found him standing in a shop doorway two nights ago, after an abortive visit to the darkroom at the Bear and Whippet. Alan wouldn't have known what a darkroom was, but he'd been given the name of the pub by the lad sitting next to him on the coach down from Carlisle, which is why he'd been standing in the shop doorway in the first place – plucking up the courage to go in. Victor had come to his rescue.

Simon Daly was the third member of the party at table five, and his partner Ronnie, the fourth. They had met ten years ago in a cottage – a public lavatory in North London – when Simon was eighteen and on his way home from an unsuccessful audition. Ronnie had offered him a cigarette in the dark – a whispered invitation to his place round the corner – and with nothing more to go on than the glint of a cigarette case, he had gone.

At eighteen – as now – the thrill for Simon had been in the chase, and when Ronnie stopped outside a large Victorian house not from where they'd met, Simon's trembling fingers let his cigarette slip. He bent down to pick it up, but before he could get hold of it, Ronnie's shiny toecap was grinding it into the pavement, and he was reaching into his overcoat pocket for another one. How sophisticated! Now Simon blushed at the very thought of it, but at the time he had viewed the whole scene as if through the lens of an old movie-camera: rain-spattered paving stones, damp brick walls and a halo of mist around the street lamp outside a Victorian terrace. The name Svengali sprang to mind.

But Ronnie's name was Delaney, as in the unacknowledged third director of the famous family partnership known as Delaney and Delaney, Theatrical Agents, and a Svengali he was not. He was an accountant.

Despite his long relationship with Ronnie – or perhaps because of it – Simon had never been signed up by the Delaneys, and in fact the only other member of the family he ever came into contact with was Ronnie's mother, Queenie.

Victor Andrews was Simon's agent, and had been for as long as either of them could remember, but it was only now, after years of signing on and the odd provincial panto, that at last their mutual loyalty was beginning to show signs of paying off. Simon was about to take the lead in a made-for-television adaptation of Sidney Taylor's *Naval Reserve,* playing Buster Sergeant, the very role that had catapulted Timothy Court to stardom long ago; and both he and Victor were hoping that history was about to repeat itself. Filming was due to start the week after next.

The evening had not been planned this way – in fact Simon had booked a table for two, with the specific intention of discussing his future with Ronnie – but Victor had spotted them arriving, and invited them to join him and Alan, leaving Simon with little choice but to pretend to be as pleased as Ronnie clearly was – or give himself away.

He tried so hard, poor Simon, not to mind that he lived in a world where the only standard was youth, but with every day that went by he found himself minding more. At twenty-eight he could still be made up to look like a teenager for the stage and screen – for the lead in *Naval Reserve*, for instance – but that was only make-believe. Off the set he looked twenty-eight, and for twenty-eight he looked good: he had a fine physique, which he worked hard to keep in shape, and in a lot of ways he was his own ideal; but to those people that mattered – to the only people his obsessive mind allowed to matter – he was already past it, and keeping the company he did, he inevitably found himself envying the Alans of this world, and the power they wielded over the likes of Ronnie and Victor – the sort of power he had once wielded himself.

He never gave up the fight – to overcome his obsession, that is. He even tried to draw comfort from the fact that Alan's own youthful looks couldn't last forever – come to think of it, Alan was the sort that ran to seed very quickly – but it was no good. Ronnie had long since stopped looking at him the way he kept looking at Alan this evening, and whatever else Simon thought of Ronnie – however little he cared for the man after all this time – that look still caused him pain.

Ronnie was telling Alan the story of how he had discovered Timothy Court, a story he had repeated so often he probably believed it himself by now, when the truth was that Tim had been signed up by the family long before Ronnie ever clapped eyes on him.

"What made you go and see him in the first place?" Alan asked.

"Intuition, I guess," said Ronnie, as if imbuing the word with a new and magical meaning. "But I could sense something special was about to happen the minute the lights went down, and…"

It was all Simon could do not to snarl. He knew Ronnie's entire repertoire by now, and had become more or less resigned to it over the years, but there was something reverential about his tone when he talked about Tim – something not unrelated to the tone he was taking with Alan now – and it never failed to get under Simon's skin.

Victor clicked his fingers for more drinks, and Alan breathed a sigh of relief, which had nothing to do with the unwelcome attention he'd been receiving from the old boy Victor had invited to join them – or the fact that it was obviously irritating his friend. A bit of a moody bastard, that one, which was a pity, because there wasn't much else wrong with him. No, the fact was that young Alan knew all too well how his night was going to end, and as small a price as that was to pay for tonight's meal and all the other treats he had signed up to in a shop doorway two nights ago, the more vodka he could get down his neck now, the more palatable would be his inevitable dessert.

Simon accepted his brandy without a word. He'd rather have left, of course, but he was buggered if he was going to be left without a drink if they were staying, and Ronnie's verbal assault on Alan was showing no sign of abating. If only he'd booked somewhere else. Come to think of it, why hadn't Victor mentioned he was coming here, when they'd spoken on the phone earlier?

Victor got up to go to the toilet, and Simon was just about to follow him, when Ronnie's mobile phone started ringing. Simon hung on to see who it was, but the signal was breaking up, and Ronnie was forced to go out into the street to take the call. That left Simon and Alan alone at the table together, neither having said more than half a dozen words to the other all evening.

In Alan's case this had been lack of opportunity rather than inclination, and with three large vodkas and several glasses of wine under his belt, he wasn't going to waste any more time now.

"I hope you didn't mind Vic asking you to sit with us?" he said.

"Not at all," said Simon, who would have died rather than admit to Alan what he really minded.

"So you're not upset, then?"

"No…why?"

"No particular reason. You've just been a bit quiet, that's all…your dad's got a lot to say for himself, though, hasn't he?"

"My dad…?" said Simon, following Alan's gaze to where Ronnie was pacing up and down on the pavement outside.

Victor reappeared, complaining loudly about the state of the lighting in the gents' toilets, and threatening to sue the man responsible for defamation of character.

Simon seemed to find that funnier than it actually was, and he was still chuckling about it when Ronnie came back in, looking as if nothing anyone could say or do would ever make him laugh again.

"I'm afraid I've got some bad news," he said, and Simon immediately jumped to the wrong conclusion.

"Oh, no," he said. "It's not your mother, is it?"

But Ronnie shook his head.

"No…no…it's not mother," he said. "It's Tim Court. He's dead."

In the stunned silence that followed, Simon bowed his head, and said:

"Well, thank God for that!"

But then, realising his mistake, he quickly added:

"No, no! I didn't mean that. I meant, thank God it wasn't Queenie!"

Trish, Louise…

Patricia and Louise Court were sitting in dressing gowns and slippers, facing each other across Trish's kitchen table, where they'd been for the best part of an hour. The table told its own story, an empty coffee pot standing over two half-empty cups, their lips growing sticky with drops of coffee; an ashtray overflowing between them, its contents mixing with the rings of moisture on the table's surface, and forming dark circles there. Louise's eyes were beginning to sting.

"Poor Esther," she said, for the third time in as many minutes. "Do you think we ought to phone her?"

"What, at this time of night?" said Trish, and then more kindly: "No…no. I think we'd better wait till morning."

Both in their seventies now, Timothy Court's paternal aunts were veterans of a more glamorous Hollywood than he had been old enough to remember – and a recent publication had famously claimed that there hadn't been a single moment during the past ten years when one of their films was not being screened on television somewhere in the world.

Trish's speciality had been suffering with stoicism, and for twenty-odd years she had reigned supreme as the undisputed queen of the American disaster movie. She'd also played an important part in Louise's success, by putting her in the frame, when she'd heard that one of the major studios was searching for a sharp looker with a snappy line in backchat. Louise had delivered with undisguised relish, and fixed herself forever in the public mind as a man-hungry temptress, who was never at a loss for something clever to say.

Unfortunately this idea had spilled over into her private life too, and to date three husbands had waited in vain for the woman they thought they'd married to emerge. Even now number four was beginning to have his doubts. Max was his name, and he and Louise lived in Palm Springs, where she had left him to ponder her fate while she flew home for a month's holiday.

Trish had been back in England thirty years now, and these days she lived in London, where she was best known as the plump grey-haired farmer's wife in a series of television ads promoting a range of organic produce. Marjorie Willow – no padding required.

Louise, on the other hand, was still as lean as ever – and the epitome of glamour, with a new outfit for every occasion. She was still a regular target for the tabloid diarists too, but these days, she couldn't help noticing, they always found it necessary to mention her age.

'*Louise Court, 70,*' it would announce under her picture, at a charity ball, say, or a gala performance; or '*70-year old*

Miss Court arriving home last night.' What were they trying to say? That she deserved their readers' sympathy for having made the effort, when she could have stayed in with her feet up?

"Did you like Tim?" she said to Trish now.

"Yes, of course," said Trish. "What little I saw of him. Why...didn't you?"

"Yes, I did...very much. I'm not so sure about Heather, though."

"I didn't know you'd met her."

"I haven't...but Esther's letters are more revealing than she realises."

"Does Esther still write to you, then?"

"Now and then, yes...or at least she did until she ran off with that Dave person. Have *you* heard from her at all?"

"Not a word. But never mind that for a minute. What did she say about Heather?"

"Oh, nothing specific. But I get the impression she thinks she's a bit of a gold digger."

"I see..."

"...And reading between the lines, I think there's a bit of resentment there too...on Heather's part, I mean."

"Resentment of who? Esther...?"

"No...Tim...and I'll bet there are a few other people in the industry who won't be sorry to see the back of him either. There's nothing like a bit of honest success to bring out the green-eyed monster in one's so-called friends."

"Oh, here we go," said Trish, getting up to refresh the pot. "We don't even know how he died yet, and you've already got the suspects queuing round the block!"

Belinda, Jack…

Belinda Lucas got out of bed and stood up to examine herself in the mirror. She was pregnant, although it didn't show yet, and so far she hadn't told her husband.

Jack came into the room, giving his belly a final rub with a small hand towel.

"I'll have to have words with Nobby," he said. "I can't find a decent towel any…"

He was brought up short by the sight of Belinda's reflection in the mirror.

"What's up?" he said.

"Eh…? Oh, nothing, really," she said. "I was just thinking about the baby, and how I'm going to tell Rod, and…" catching a glimpse of Jack's naked body, "…well, you know…Anyway, come on, we'd better get going, or we'll both be in trouble."

Half an hour later Belinda was driving too fast along Kensington High Street, having dropped Jack home first, the latest – and last – in a long line of leading men; or so Belinda told herself now, with two weeks of the play still to run.

She had recently read that it was possible to become addicted to sex, in much the same way as it is to alcohol and drugs, and she did sometimes wonder if that was what had happened to her. She had certainly become more obsessive about it over the past couple of years – the couple of years since Timothy Court had come into her life, as it happens – but did that amount to an addiction? She always felt terribly guilty afterwards, but the trouble was that when it came to the point of calling a halt, she had so many previous indiscretions to take into account, the idea of one more never seemed to make much difference. If only she could wipe the slate clean.

With a bit of luck and a favourable weather forecast, Rodney would be asleep when she got home – ready for golf in the morning – because although he had never succeeded in catching her out yet, there was always a danger that if he came too close too soon, he might be able to sense what she'd been up to – to smell it on her. Thank God he took his golf as seriously as his job.

He worked in the City, where losing wasn't an option, and three times a week he worked out in a gym with a wall-sized mirror that made the place look twice as big as it was – and twice as well-equipped too.

Nobody would have dared call Rodney insecure – not to his face anyway – and in fact it probably wasn't the first word most people would have chosen to describe him; but you have to work hard at being manly, and sometimes Rodney even practised shaking hands with himself to make sure his grip was as firm as he wanted it to be. It's difficult to tell though – shaking hands with yourself – which is probably why he always overdid the real thing. He drove a Porsche these days, having traded in his Mercedes Sports when it was just three weeks old, after hearing one complete stranger describing it to another as 'a poof's motor'.

Belinda had met him at a charity do, and still swore she'd only married him because he looked good in a tuxedo, when the truth was that he reminded her of her father, a man she had spent a lifetime plotting to escape, only to have him die on her unexpectedly, and leave her without a purpose.

Like her father, Rodney had turned out to be fiercely protective of her, while in constant need of reassurance that she was worthy of his trust. It could be quite wearing, actually, particularly in company.

Fortunately for Belinda, Rodney didn't have much time for her friends, but there were occasions when he was obliged to accompany her to some function or other – an awards dinner, or a first night, perhaps – and over the years he had been introduced to several of her lovers, albeit without knowing it.

Any number of people could have enlightened him there, including Timothy Court – although in Tim's case nothing had come of Belinda's approach. He had turned her down politely, and never referred to the matter again, but it had made him wonder if some of the stories he'd heard about her were true, and – knowing Rodney – that made him uneasy.

Belinda wasn't exactly feeling fully at ease herself, driving home in the early hours after a heavy session with Jack; and it didn't help matters when she turned into the drive and saw that there was still a light on in the front room. Rodney hadn't gone to bed after all. But she needn't have worried. He was only waiting up to tell her the news.

Jack, Moira…

The bedroom was in darkness, and Jack's wife, Moira was lying on her side, her back towards the door as usual. She could smell the scotch on Jack's breath the minute he came in, and she stiffened, so as not to show the slightest sign of life while he undressed.

But it was different tonight. Usually Jack swallowed his drink downstairs in order to prepare himself for the trial by silence that inevitably followed; but tonight he'd brought his glass with him.

He climbed on to the bed, and whispered gently into her ear:

"Darling, are you still awake?"

"Of course I'm still awake!" she thought. "I'm always still awake…!" But she didn't say a word.

"Moira…? Have you heard about Timothy Court…?"

It was such an unexpected question, Moira couldn't help but be interested. She turned to face her husband.

"He's dead," said Jack. "I've just heard it on the radio."

Dave…

David Savage often joked that his car knew its own way home from the Regent – particularly when one of his mates looked like leaving him out of the round – but, joking apart, a decent car was essential to him in his line of business, and the Mondeo was never going to get through its MOT, the state it was in. What he couldn't understand was why Esther hadn't come up with the cash for a new one. He'd dropped enough hints, for Christ's sake.

Two o' clock. Well, at least he could have a fag in peace, without attracting one of those looks of hers, which were rapidly becoming her principal means of communication. She was bound to be in bed by now.

But when he came round the corner, the first thing he noticed was a police car parked outside his front door – and a light on in the hall.

D I Lawrence…

Detective Inspector Frank Lawrence had no idea that he had entered into a conspiracy with Heather Swallows, when she'd turned and smiled at him by the Manor House swimming pool. But that was what it amounted to.

She'd been wearing a towelling robe, and very little else, according to PC Malone, who'd been first on the scene. In fact it had been the effect her appearance was having on PC Malone that had caused her to smile at Frank in the first place – despite the tragic circumstances.

Exceptional circumstances or not? Certainly exceptional enough to have put the kibosh on a precious night in front of the television with Mrs Lawrence – and they'd been enjoying the film – but was it going to prove more than that? Detective Inspector Lawrence thought not.

This was Heather's story.

She'd had a headache. There had been no aspirins in the house, so her husband had gone to buy some for her. She'd taken two and gone to bed. That was about…half nine. At half ten she'd woken up to find the other side of the bed unoccupied, which had surprised her, because Tim had been talking about making an early night of it. So she'd gone downstairs to find him. In the bathrobe she was wearing now, yes, and the pair of briefs she'd been wearing when his colleagues arrived.

The place had been in darkness, and at first she'd thought Tim must have gone out again, but then she'd seen a light on in the pool house, and gone to investigate. She'd found him lying face down in the water.

She'd jumped in – having taken the bathrobe off first,

yes — and turned Tim over, then tried to get him out of the pool. But he was too heavy, so she'd pulled him to the edge, and propped his head against the rail, while she got out to phone an ambulance. No, she wasn't sure if he'd still been alive at that point…but she couldn't do nothing, could she?

So she'd dialled 999, and then jumped back into the pool before she could be put through, because Tim's head had slipped off the rail, and he was rolling over on to his face again. After that, she had stayed with him until the ambulance arrived.

No, she was sure nobody else had been in the house. The patio doors had been locked on the inside, the key still in the door. In fact she'd thought of that while she was phoning the ambulance, and unlocked it at the same time. A cordless phone, yes…

Tim had obviously gone into the pool intentionally — he'd been wearing his trunks — but he'd never been a good swimmer. In fact Heather had only found out recently that her husband couldn't swim at all, and had insisted on teaching him herself.

He hadn't had a drink, no…oh, possibly a glass of wine at lunchtime.

Heather's unguarded answers had satisfied the policeman, and he very much doubted that forensics would come up with anything to challenge them. There would have to be a post mortem, of course, and there was some CCTV footage of the exterior to check. The security cameras inside the Manor House only cut in when the alarm was switched on, so nothing doing there, but D I Lawrence was convinced that if they had been recording, it would have been exactly the sequence of events Heather had described earlier. And the self-conscious smile she'd directed at him then had only confirmed what he already knew – that he understood women better than any other man on the force.

On his way home, DC Cooper had called him to say the news was out, despite his assurance that he would keep it under wraps until the dead man's mother had been informed; but that didn't change anything.

On Monday the coroner would release Timothy Court's body for burial on the recommendation of Detective Inspector Frank Lawrence – and all because of one smile.

SATURDAY, 18

8th February 1937

SEVEN KILLED IN FIRE

A five-year old boy was left orphaned yesterday, when fire swept through a lodging house in Adelaide Street, killing all seven occupants. The blaze is believed to have started in a ground floor room at the back of the house, where...

Agatha Jemison lived alone. Harold and his parents lived in the room directly above hers, but she moved about so little they would hardly have known she was there.

No television in those days, of course – not even a radio as far as Harold could remember – just the sound of his parents' lowered voices behind the curtain his father had rigged up at the end of his bed to help him sleep; the creak of a floorboard above; a dog's bark; a shout in the street below.

The front door was always open during the day; and outside there was a narrow concreted area under the bay window, a low wall in front of that.

When the present day Harold was feeling sorry for himself, he sometimes conjured up an image of a solitary little figure sitting on that wall, watching the other kids play. But like the women's doorstep conversations and the men getting drunk in the pub on the corner, it wasn't actually a memory at all – just a lonely man's idea of what it must have been like. No walks in the park, no trips to the cinema, no treats…

Yes, one regular treat – thick slices of bread toasted on Aggie's open fire, Aggie sitting too close, her legs mottled by the heat. She would offer it as a reward for going to the corner shop for her. Never any question of his not being allowed to go as far as the shops on his own, even at the age of five…

Until one day he came back to find the house ablaze, flames leaping out of every window, men and women running up and down the street with buckets of water. No sign of Aggie or his mother or father.

Before he could come to terms with what was happening, kind hands were steering him away from the scene, and with one final look over his shoulder, he brought the first chapter of his life to an end. Just like that.

Now Tim is dead. It's four o' clock in the morning, and Harold hasn't moved since Cassie tried to peep in at his window last night. He doesn't own a television or a phone or a radio, and he hasn't heard a sound in hours – not a creak, not a bark, not a whisper. In fact the last thing he remembers hearing is Cassie's confused reply when he asked her to leave him alone.

"But…?"

He knows Tim is dead…

...And if the security cameras inside the Manor House had been switched on at ten o'clock last night, the policeman checking the footage this morning would have recognised Tim's body floating face down in the pool. But he'd also have noticed it was fully clothed. Fast forward a few seconds, and Heather would appear in the pool alongside her husband. But she wouldn't turn him over or try and revive him. She'd tow him to the shallow end, and start undressing him. Shoes, socks, trousers, shirt – item by item she'd methodically remove them all, and pile them up on the edge of the pool, until Tim was wearing nothing but the swimming trunks he'd be wearing when the ambulance arrived an hour later. Then Heather would climb out of the water, gather up the evidence, and disappear into the house.

Switch to the master bedroom, where Heather could be found a few minutes later, lying on the bed with her eyes closed, while somewhere not far away a washing machine went through its rinse and spin cycle.

If only the security cameras had been switched on.

Victor...

Victor knew a lot about Simon's relationship with Ronnie. How they'd met, for instance – in a cottage not far from Ronnie's old shag pad in Victoria Terrace – and how Simon had decided to take a chance in the dark.

The sex wasn't much good – in fact it was more or less non-existent these days, but it had never been much good as far as Victor knew, and according to a recent drunken confidence, it had only been the intensity of Ronnie's need that had sustained Simon's interest beyond the first grope.

They'd always slept in separate rooms, which suited Simon fine, or so he said, but over the years the knocks on his door had grown fewer and further between – and then dried up altogether – which hadn't done a lot for his fragile self-image. So he'd turned to his best friend for reassurance.

It was with all this in mind that Victor had booked a table at Alfredo's last night, having heard from Simon earlier that he and Ronnie were intending to eat there themselves. He wanted to show Alan off, and if that involved reminding his friends of what was lacking in their own lives, well…so much the better.

He hadn't set foot in his office for days now – since Wednesday, in fact, when he'd been lucky enough to discover Alan in a shop doorway opposite the Bear and Whippet – and he'd been hoping to make a long weekend of it. But last night's news had changed all that. As the morning wore on, the world of entertainment would be waking up to its loss, and as Tim Court's agent, it wouldn't be long before his phone started ringing. So he decided to go in.

It did cross his mind briefly that he was taking a bit of a chance leaving a comparative stranger alone in his flat, but the boy seemed honest enough, and – more important – willing enough, so he took him tea in bed, and told him to make himself at home.

Esther…

Esther took Ben out at the same time every morning –

because that was what Oliver had insisted on when they bought him as a puppy.

"The most important thing in a dog's life is routine," he'd said, before going on to remind her what a busy man he was, and his meaning had been so clear, she'd laughed and said:

"Don't worry. You just help me choose one, and I'll take care of the rest. Promise."

Which is why she was walking Ben along Hove Lawns at 8.30 this morning, despite the devastating news. Esther never broke a promise.

Ironic, though, that Oliver was still getting his own way even now, and Esther did sometimes wonder if her adventure with Dave had been a subconscious act of defiance.

Her adventure! What a joke! But that must have been how she'd thought of it when it started. Or what was she doing in Brighton at all?

The idea had been that she would stay with Tim and Heather if the Hampstead house sold before she found somewhere else to live, but in the event Tim had been abroad filming, and Esther hadn't fancied being holed up in Denby Green with no one but Heather for company. So she'd fallen in with Dave's suggestion, and rented a small house in Brighton. A small, three-bedroomed house.

A few days after she'd moved in, a van had pulled up outside her front door, and Esther had walked out to find a man wiring a 'FOR SALE' sign to her railings. Next thing her landlord had rolled up too, although he didn't look much like a landlord to her. He was younger than Tim.

He introduced himself as Clive Wolstenholme, and told her he'd bought the house years ago – as an investment, he said, but he earned his living running an art gallery in The Lanes. At least he had until now. Now an opportunity had come up to indulge his other passion – animal rights – and he was intending to open a donkey sanctuary in Madrid. But he needed some capital, which is why he was selling up.

He told Esther all this over coffee at her kitchen table, and she felt so comfortable in his company, that when he said he'd deduct six months' rent from the asking price if she fancied buying the place herself, she was tempted to say yes, just to see his reaction. But that wouldn't have been fair, so she thanked him and said no.

"Nine months, then," he said. "You drive a hard bargain."

And this time she laughed and said:

"But I've only rented it for three."

"I know," he said, grinning. "I'm your landlord, remember? But the agent did happen to mention you were looking for somewhere to buy, so I thought I'd give you first refusal. Buy the place now, and save yourself three times what you're paying me in rent. Then, if by next summer you haven't fallen totally in love with it – sell it again. Prices are on the way up. I don't see how you can lose."

Put like that, it did sound like a bargain, and Esther half wished Dave was there to advise her. But he was having lunch with his ex-wife, Sylvia. So she took the decision herself.

When Dave came round that evening to take her out for dinner, he seemed a bit quiet, so despite the fact that she was dying to tell him her news, she asked him if he'd rather leave it, and go out another night. But he wanted to talk, he said, so they went to Carlo's as planned. And he gave it to her straight.

Sylvia was threatening to take him to court, because he hadn't been able to come up with the cash he'd promised her when they split up.

"That's on top of the house, by the way," he explained. "Oh, and the car, of course, which is why I'm driving round in that clapped out Mondeo. Anyway, the point is, I'm going to have to get myself a solicitor, and the way business has been going lately, I'm not even sure how I'm going to pay for that. I can hardly afford my rent, to be honest."

By the time Esther exchanged contracts on her new home, Dave had already been living there for the best part of a month, but in a room of his own, having tactfully broached the subject of sleeping arrangements before he moved in.

Now, four months later, and having married her in the meantime, he still hadn't touched her – or at least not in the way she'd once hoped he would. In fact he'd never even invited her into his room. At first she'd thought he was holding back out of respect for Oliver's memory, but the truth was he had only married her for her money. Not that that mattered now. Nothing mattered any more – apart from Ben's routine.

Heather, Gerry…

It was hours now since Tim's body had been removed to

the mortuary, and Heather was standing at her bedroom window, wondering how she was going to get through the next few days without giving herself away – although she did think the interview with Detective Inspector Lawrence had gone well. There would be no fooling her brother, Gerry – in fact she was secretly looking forward to letting him tease the truth out of her – but what about the rest of them? What about Tim's friends and family? What about Esther?

Sooner or later she was going to have to face them all – at the funeral, for instance, when they'd be together for the first time since the wedding, and the world's media would be descending on Denby Green again. But what would they be expecting?

A fleet of stately limousines? Or a horse drawn hearse? A glass-sided carriage, perhaps, with TIMOTHY spelt out in white carnations along the side of the coffin inside it. Esther would be hoping for something simple and discreet – a family affair behind closed doors – but it would be up to Heather to decide, of course, and the point was that whatever she chose, all eyes were going to be on her at every tearful turn in the proceedings. Someone was bound to see through her.

Unless, that is, she adapted the general mood to her own, instead of the other way round. Give them something to smile about. After all, if you hide a tree in a forest, where better to hide your good humour than in a sea of smiling faces? The question was – how to go about it?

The Manor House was surrounded on three sides by about two-and-a-half acres of garden, but this side of the house looked straight down on to the lane, separated from it by a narrow border, which was planted with dozens of daffodils. Tim had often told her they were his favourite flowers.

It must have been the breeze that set up an uneasy stir there, but at the same moment, Heather was distracted by a movement in the lane. A man was walking by.

He looked for all the world like a figure out of a Wild West film – one of those colourful confidence tricksters, who travel round the country selling bottled cures and Bible talk to gullible townsfolk. He was wearing grey pinstriped trousers, a white cotton shirt, a black string tie, a bowler hat and an embroidered waistcoat in dazzling gold silk. But what was he doing in Manor House Lane?

Whatever it was, it could hardly have been more timely as far as Heather was concerned, because it was his appearance that provided her with the answer to her problem. And the answer was in colour.

Not just the colour of the daffodils that would be arriving in their thousands, once she put the word about that they were Tim's favourite flowers, but in the bright colours she would insist the mourners wore to Tim's funeral, to comply with his wishes. Tim hadn't expected to die so young, of course, but in his own thoughtful way, he'd left instructions just in case; and in death, as in life, all he wanted was for everyone to be happy. Even Esther wouldn't be able to argue with that.

Heather was smiling a silent thank you to the brightly dressed man in the lane, when suddenly he looked up at her, and caught her in the act. Or at least that was how it felt, despite his blank expression – as if he knew exactly what she'd been thinking. Her instinctive response was to duck away from the window – too quickly, it occurred to her from her refuge behind the curtain – but when she tried to make amends, it was too late. He had gone.

"He was probably a pap," said Gerry, through a mouthful of toast. She had found him in the kitchen, where he was tucking into breakfast, having been summoned to the Manor House last night at Inspector Lawrence's insistence.

"I didn't see a camera," she said. "And anyway, apart from the way he was dressed, what would a pap be doing here at this time of the morning?"

And then it hit her.

Detective Inspector Lawrence had promised her he would do all he could to keep the story of Tim's death quiet, at least until Esther had been informed. He'd said he would arrange for a couple of officers to call at her house and give her the news in person – which Heather had taken to mean some time this morning. But what if the police took a different view? What if they had sent someone round straight away?

She looked at the clock and said:

"You don't think the press have got hold of this already, do you?"

Gerry looked genuinely surprised.

"Well, of course they have," he said. "Didn't I tell you?"

"Tell me what?" said Heather.

"I phoned Guy Blakely last night before I came over."

"You did what?"

"Well, if I hadn't, somebody else would have, wouldn't they? And you don't get any medals for coming second, do you?"

Heather the competitive swimmer could have argued with that – in fact, Heather could have argued with a lot of things her brother said – but what was the point? She loved him for what he was, not what he should have been, and he had done the obvious thing for him, by getting in first with the news, and putting a useful media hound in his debt.

No, there was no point in getting angry with him, so Heather did the next best thing, and – forgetting all about the mystery man in the lane – she went to phone her mother-in-law, while Gerry finished his breakfast.

Esther…

The first time Esther had ever picked up a mobile phone was when Dave proposed. They were in a taxi at the time, and Esther wanted to tell Tim the news straight away; so Dave offered her his mobile, and then had to show her how to use it. But while it was ringing, she remembered Tim was in France, and it would be Heather who answered, so she asked Dave to switch it off…quickly…quickly…

The second time was a couple of months after the wedding. They were at home this time, and Dave's mobile rang one morning while he was having a shower, so she tracked it down to his bedside table, and tentatively pressed the button marked 'Reply'.

"Hello?"

"Oh," said a woman's voice. "I think I may have the wrong number. Is that Dave Savage's phone?"

"Yes, it is," said Esther. "But I'm afraid he's in the shower at the moment."

"Oh, is he now?" said the woman. "And who might you be?"

But before she could reply, Dave appeared in the doorway, wearing nothing but his Y-fronts, and trembling with fury.

"What the hell do you think you're doing?" he said, and then came at her so ferociously, she actually thought he was going to hit her. But instead he grabbed her wrist, and snatched the phone out of her hand, before pulling her towards him, so that their faces were nearly touching.

"Never…ever do that again," he said, dragging her out of his room, and slamming the door behind her. Then he stormed back into the bathroom, and she crossed the landing to her own bedroom, where she stayed until he went out.

Later he brought her flowers, but there was no apology or explanation, and he didn't seem to expect one from her, although by this time she'd half convinced herself he was due one. Perhaps she had overstepped the mark by going into his room uninvited…answering his phone. She would have liked to talk about it, but he was behaving as if nothing had happened, and there was no one else to talk to, so she decided to leave well alone, and be more careful in future.

The following day, she was out walking Ben, when a woman overtook her, and stopped to admire him.

"Lovely dog," she said.

"Thank you," said Esther.

"I used to have a lab myself. What's his name?"

"Ben."

"Very wise," said the woman, crouching down to give his ears a rub. "A name you can shout in public, without making a fool of yourself."

Then she looked up at Esther's face, and said:
"I'm Sylvia, by the way."

It turned out she'd followed Esther all the way from home, trying to make up her mind how to approach her without scaring her off. She'd been watching the house from her car for the best part of an hour, having followed Dave home from the pub the night before. She knew where he drank, and the sort of hours he kept, so it hadn't been difficult; and, in fact she'd been hoping he'd be the first to go out this morning, so she could knock and introduce herself in a more straightforward way. But this was better really. Less chance of being caught red-handed. And somehow Esther felt the same, despite the fact that she'd played no part in the conspiracy. Because it wasn't just the name she recognised.

"It was you…on the phone…" she said.

"Yes," said Sylvia.

Ten minutes later they were sitting in a café under Kings Road arches, at a table in the window, so that Esther could keep an eye on Ben, who was tethered to a railing outside.

"I'm sorry I spoke to you like that," said Sylvia. "Yesterday, I mean…on the phone. It was just that I had visions of some tart in a seedy hotel somewhere, helping him spend my money. And then…well, I heard his voice, and it brought it all back."

The money Dave owed her was nothing to do with a divorce settlement. They'd never been married. It was just her share of the joint account he'd emptied the day she threw him out. Or at least the day her nephew threw him out for her. Andy. He and his boyfriend, Dan had moved in with her now, and it was the best decision she'd ever made. Real men, she said defiantly, and there was no need to explain.

The house had been hers long before she met Dave, and as for the car, the Mondeo was the only car they'd ever possessed as a couple. She'd bought it for him as a moving in present.

That was what she told Esther, anyway, and Esther was inclined to believe her. But then she'd believed Dave until yesterday.

A young man walked past outside, and Esther did a double take.

"Clive Wolstenholme," said Sylvia.

"Yes, of course," said Esther. "…Clive. Do you know him then?"

"Oh yes," said Sylvia. "Everyone knows Clive. Well, everyone who's been in Brighton any length of time, anyway. He's a vulture. Makes his money out of other people's misery. You know, bankrupt stock, repossessions, that sort of thing? Why? How do you know him?"

"He sold me my house."

All heads turned towards the table in the window, and the sudden outburst of laughter from the two women sitting there; until it gradually subsided…only to erupt again, when the older of the two leaned over to her friend and said something they apparently found even more hilarious.

"What was all that about?" said one of the regulars to the waitress afterwards.

"Well, I didn't catch the full story," said the waitress. "But it was something to do with a donkey sanctuary in Madrid."

Esther had a mobile of her own these days. Tim had bought it for her a few weeks ago, and she'd accepted it on the understanding that it was only to be used in emergencies. So it had never rung – until now.

Belinda, Rodney…

"Who was that on the phone, darling?"

The question sounded innocent enough, but it was an irritating fact of Belinda's life with Rodney, that he spent almost as much time challenging her with his suspicions, as she did giving him reason to – and Gerry Swallows was not a name he would be happy to hear.

Still, he was going to have to be told, because it had been Gerry on the phone, and besides, Gerry was safe ground as far as Belinda was concerned, in that he was single, and she never strayed from the rules of her game – married men only.

"What did he want?" said Rodney.

"*He* didn't want anything," said Belinda. "It was me that phoned Heather actually…to offer her our condolences."

"So what were you doing talking to Gerry?"

"Oh, for Christ's sake, Rod, he answered the phone, that's all! What was I supposed to do? Hang up?"

It was a scene the two had acted out a hundred times before, and the wounded look that appeared on Rodney's face now, was Belinda's cue to comfort him with a word or two of reassurance. But an idea had been taking shape in her mind all morning – a way of using last night's events to boost the sales of her forthcoming autobiography – and perhaps this was as good a time as any to test the water.

"It's funny, really," she said, as if it was hardly worth the mention.

"What is?" said Rodney. This wasn't part of the script.

"That of all the men who've ever tried it on with me…"

"Ah, so you admit he's tried it on with you, then?"

"No, not Gerry, you twit…Tim."

"Tim? What, Tim Court, you mean?"

"Yes, Tim Court. Don't sound so surprised."

"When?"

"A couple of years ago. The first time we worked together actually."

"What happened?"

"Well, one of the crew had found this little restaurant in the mountains, you see, and…"

"Never mind all that. What happened?"

"Nothing. How many times have I got to tell you…?"

"Why haven't you mentioned it before then?"

"Why do you think? You'd have been over there like a shot, making a complete bloody fool of yourself. Anyway, never mind that now. Why don't you pour yourself a nice little drinky and come upstairs with me? I've got something much more important to tell you."

Belinda had been hoping to buy herself a few more precious seconds, but Rodney had never been renowned for his patience, and he stood in her way.

"Tell me now," he said.

"All right," she said. Come to think of it, there weren't that many ways of saying it: "I'm pregnant."

But which way was he going to jump?

For a moment she was tempted to get her protest in

first – "…And before you ask, yes, I am sure it's yours…" – that sort of thing – but if experience had taught her to stick to the truth whenever possible, it had also taught her not to elaborate on the lie; and she had already said it once today: "How many times have I got to tell you…?"

"Are you sure?" said Rodney.

"What…? Oh, about being pregnant? Yes, of course…"

"I…I don't know what to say."

"Then don't say anything. Just give me a kiss and let me get on, or I'm going to be late."

"Late? You're not still going to work, surely?"

"I most certainly am. And you, my little daddy to be, are just going to have to get used to the idea."

Trish, Louise…

"And by the time they got to Esther, it was too late," said Trish, but Louise was too absorbed to take in what she was saying. She was watching the one o' clock news.

"You see, the police said they wouldn't release the news until this morning," said Trish. "But someone must have let the cat out of the bag before they even left the house, because they didn't leave till after twelve, and even we'd heard about it by then, hadn't we…? Lou!"

"Shoosh a minute. I'm trying to listen."

It was an item about Tim, and Belinda Lucas was on screen, talking about her shock at his loss, and the fact that although they had only worked together a couple of times, there had always been this incredible tension between them…

The eyes dipped, the voice faltered, and the suggestion hovered in the air that perhaps there had been more to

Belinda's relationship with Tim than met the eye. Louise didn't believe it for a minute, but then Louise wasn't in a position to give her opinion.

Cassie...

'I was like a rabbit caught in a car's headlights,' Cassie wrote in her diary...

> And Harold was the driver who stopped just in time.
> He said he'd been having a bad dream, which – now that I come to think of it – must have been round about the time Tim was drowning. But of course I didn't know that then. So when he asked me to leave him alone – I did. And a couple of hours later they announced it on TV.
> I went back to tell him, but when I knocked there was no answer, so I kept watch at my window until about four, when I gave up and went to bed. He must have slipped the note under my door while I was asleep.
> It said he'd heard the news, and that I was not to change my plans under any circumstances, because he was taking himself out of circulation for a while, to give himself time to reflect and make up his mind what to do. Sounds ominous. He never leaves this place except to drive round the lanes of Kent in that souped up motor of his...like some demented Toad.
> Anyway, he hasn't gone anywhere – unless he's been and come back again – because I saw him an hour ago, climbing over the fence into the top field. I don't think he saw me, so I didn't call out to him. I just followed

> him at a distance until he sat down under the big horse
> chestnut in the corner – and then left him to it.
> Funny about that dream, though.

Simon, Ronnie…

Simon and Ronnie were in the middle of dinner. Simon had spent a very edgy day in town, going over last night's visit to Alfredo's detail by minute detail, and looking forward to the good stiff drink he would pour himself when he got home. Now, several dry martinis down the line, he was washing down a small portion of one of Judith's delicious steak and kidney pies with two or three glasses of the usual St Emilion. 'A very drinkable little claret' was how Ronnie always described it, which meant it was cheap, but Simon couldn't have cared less as long as it was there. After the day he'd had it was a drink he was in need of, not an epicurean experience. A very drinkable little claret – Ronnie could be so pompous sometimes.

Ronnie was saying how thoughtful it had been of Heather to phone him this morning, which wasn't quite true, as he had phoned her, but Simon wasn't to know that, any more than he was to know the price of the wine.

"Poor woman," spluttered Simon, through a mouthful of pie. "It must have come as a bit of a shock to her to discover she'd been living with a mere mortal all these years."

"What's that supposed to mean?" said Ronnie.

"Oh, take no notice. I just don't seem to be able to get

away from him lately, that's all. And, of course, now that he's dead…I heard two women talking about him in the paper shop this morning, and one of them said it was the best career move he'd made in years."

"Really?" said Ronnie. "And I suppose you thought that was funny, did you?"

"Yes, I did actually," said Simon.

"Well, it isn't," said Ronnie. "It isn't funny, it isn't original, and it certainly isn't true."

"Suit yourself."

But it wasn't in Ronnie's nature just to leave it at that.

"You know what your trouble is, don't you?" he said.

"No…what?"

"You're jealous."

"Me? Jealous? What have I got to be jealous of?"

"Oh, come on, Simon. I've only got to mention Tim's name, and you're practically tearing up the carpet."

"Doesn't stop you doing it, I notice. And anyway, that's not jealousy. It's frustration at having to listen to the drivel you talk about him."

"Drivel, is it? Well, in that case I think it might just be time to let you in on our little secret."

"Whose secret?"

"Mine and Tim's. I take it you remember my old place in Victoria Terrace?"

"Of course."

"Good. And why do you think I bought it, Simon? On the off-chance of bumping into you in some cottage?"

One more stain on the wall behind Ronnie's left ear, one less plate for Judith to wash up, and once again tomorrow morning it would be Simon's conscience cleaving him to the bedclothes, while Ronnie started his day the way he started every day – with a clean slate and a hearty breakfast.

Alan…

Alan was in one of those reflective moods that usually left him wondering if he was going to end up like his mother – a sad case. He was drinking vodka.

Victor had phoned earlier to say he wouldn't be home till about nine, and the idea was that they'd stay in tonight, and phone out for a pizza; so Alan hadn't bothered to get dressed, but had spent the afternoon mooching around the flat in a dressing gown he'd found in the airing cupboard – flicking through magazines, watching television …drinking. He did have some blow in his bag, but Victor had put his foot down there – couldn't stand the smell.

The boy sitting next to Alan on the coach down from Carlisle had told him he was on the run from the police, before going on to describe what was likely to be on offer at the Bear and Whippet; and it was the conflict between those two stories that had kept him hovering in a doorway near the pub long enough for Victor to find him.

On the one hand he had been afraid to go in. He had told his mother he was going camping in the Lakes with a group of friends from school, and, however remote the possibility, he didn't want her finding out the truth. It wouldn't have crossed her mind to check up on him herself – she was far too wrapped up in her own life for that – but he was still under age – or so he thought, anyway –

and he wasn't sure what the police would do if they caught him. Would they tell her?

On the other hand it was his fantasies about the London gay scene that had brought him down here in the first place. He had a friend back home – a man called Cameron – who had this amazing collection of porn, and Alan had often wondered where the people who published it found so many good-looking men – certainly not Carlisle, anyway. Maybe the Bear and Whippet, then? He still didn't know.

What he did know was that Victor would be home soon, when it would be large vodkas and tonics, and a suggestive comment or two about what he was hiding under his dressing gown; whereas with Cameron, back in Carlisle, it was more likely to be a joint and a gentle tease about what he'd been up to with his mates at school.

He'd been 'seeing' Cameron on and off for nearly four years now. Cameron owned a tobacconist's near Alan's school, and had been smiling at him since he was twelve, biding his time until, on the very first occasion Alan had found himself alone in the shop with him, he'd given him a magazine full of pictures of men and women having sex, that he could 'have a wank over' with his friends.

Alan had been completely tongue-tied and unsure what to do, while at the same time intrigued and kind of thrilled to hear a man of Cameron's age use the word 'wank' – and Cameron had known it. They always knew, as Alan had discovered since – like a brotherhood with an unspoken understanding. Cameron had stuffed the magazine into his bag without another word, and winked at him.

The next day they had found themselves alone in the shop together again, only on this occasion it was Alan who had bided his time – waiting until the coast was clear before going in.

Was Cameron a paedophile? Or was Julius a paedophile, one of Alan's mother's ex-lovers?

Alan had had a lot in common with Julius – a love of films for one thing, and musicals in particular – but more importantly, he'd been flattered that unlike most of his mother's boyfriends, Julius had always seemed pleased to have him around. Perhaps he should have seen the signs.

Helen was drinking a lot at the time, and one day when she'd invited Julius round for a meal, she was already well gone by the time he arrived. She made it to the table where the wine continued to flow, but her food remained untouched, and by half past eight she was incoherent, and had to be put to bed.

Alan and Julius had a chuckle about it when Alan came back into the dining room five minutes later, but after that the conversation took an unnatural turn, and an air of expectation hung over the proceedings, which could only be resolved one way.

A pattern developed, which involved Helen limiting herself to two or three glasses of wine a day, except when she was going out or entertaining, of course, in which case she allowed herself as much as she liked.

Coincidentally, she started going out more, and Julius was invited for dinner at least once a week. She was a methodical cook, Helen, and every Friday at six-thirty she would disappear into the kitchen with a large gin and tonic, to be followed by another one at seven, when Julius arrived. White wine with the first course, red with the main, she never fancied a pud much, and 'the boys' were invariably asked if they minded helping themselves to coffee, while she went for a lie-down.

Alan and Julius would stay at the table for another ten minutes or so, and Julius would pour Alan a glass of wine, while they talked in lowered tones, never taking too much interest in what they were saying, but listening out for the slightest movement from the direction of Helen's bedroom, until they felt it was safe to move into the living room. Glass in hand, Alan would always check at Helen's door on the way through.

Was Julius a paedophile? Or Cameron? Or Victor for that matter? Or Ronnie, the old bore from last night, who Alan had pretended to think was Simon's father, just to make him smile. Come to think of it, though, Alan was nearly eighteen now, so perhaps the question didn't apply at all these days. What was the legal age limit? Was it sixteen? Or eighteen? And did that mean it was the law that defined what a paedophile was? Not as far as Alan was concerned, it didn't, because at fourteen – as at seventeen and a half – he had known what he was doing, and – then as now – the overriding need had been the need to be wanted at all.

Helen's current boyfriend was a born-again Christian called Vinnie. She had met him in rehab at the back end of last year, and a couple of months ago he'd moved in; but what with AA meetings and the church and his various other commitments, he didn't seem to have much time for Alan.

Trish, Louise…

Trish was about to suggest a game of cards when Louise said:

"I'm thinking of having an affair…oh, now don't look at me like that. I'm serious. I've been meaning to tell you ever since I arrived, but, what with one thing and another…"

"Who's the lucky man?"

"Um…there isn't one yet actually. In fact, I was hoping you might help me find someone."

Victor, Alan…

By the time Victor came home at a quarter past nine, Alan was ready for him, vodka glass washed and dried and back where he'd found it, alongside the bottle, which he'd topped up with half an inch of Malvern water. Of course he had been absolutely right about the effect his dressing gown would have on his host, but if Victor hadn't picked him for his grasp of psychology, that is not to say he didn't have a few ideas about what made people tick, and it was as clear to him as a pile of Victor's favourite pastries on a plate, that it was more than just the man's physical needs he was here to satisfy. Egos need feeding too, and Victor's was as big as his ever-expanding waistline.

"You look nice and cosy," said Victor, leaning over the back of the settee, and kissing him on the cheek. "What have you been up to today?"

"Oh, nothing much," he said. "Reading…nosing about. I saw you on telly this afternoon."

"Did you?" Victor sounded pleased. "How was I?"

"Pretty cool."

"Was I...? Good...good..."

Victor picked up the vodka bottle, and smiled to himself.

"Nosing about, eh?"

"Well, you did tell me to make myself at home, didn't you?"

Moments later, and it was Victor who was making himself at home – in the folds of Alan's dressing gown.

"What do you think of Belinda Lucas?" said Alan.

"Not much," said Victor. "Why?"

"Just wondered, that's all."

Victor settled back to his task.

"Only she was on telly this afternoon...just after you."

Victor looked up again. Was the boy playing for time? But he seemed willing enough, if not exactly joining in.

"Have you ever met her?" he asked now, and he did seem genuinely to want to know.

"Yes, we've crossed swords once or twice. Why?"

"What's she like?"

"Well," said Victor, getting up to pour them both a drink. "She's not exactly my cup of tea, but..."

"Is she married?"

"She is, yes...but she does put it about a bit. Why?"

"I think she might have been screwing Timothy Court."

"Never. Is that what she said?"

"Not exactly, no. But I'm sure that's what she meant."

"Well...it's possible I suppose, but I think you probably got the wrong end of the stick, to be honest. Tim was completely smitten with Heather."

"Maybe it happened before he met Heather."

"Maybe, but I doubt it. Belinda only ever fucks around with married men. Everybody knows that."

Louise, Trish…

"They lie down with Foxy Roxy and they wake up with me."

An oft-quoted line from an interview given by Louise Court some forty-odd years ago, after cleaning up at the Oscars as the scorching Roxy Fleming, only to lose out equally spectacularly in a string of short-lived love affairs. She was convinced nothing had changed.

But what about her husbands? Trish had tried to argue. Surely they had married her for the woman she really was?

Clearly not, said Louise, or there wouldn't have been so many of them. No, the husbands had just been a bit slower on the uptake than the rest; and as for Max – husband number four – well, Max was the slowest of them all. But it was only a matter of time.

That was why she had decided to have an affair, as she was explaining to Trish now – to revive Max's interest, before it was too late.

"You mean you're going to tell him?" said Trish.

"Not exactly," she said. "But I am going to let him know somehow, yes. I'm just not quite sure how yet."

Victor, Alan…

Victor was on his second vodka now, which must mean Alan was on his…fourth?

"Gerry Swallows is a bit tasty, isn't he?" he said.

"Not bad," said Victor, and his thoughts raced to a drawer in his bedside table, where there was a pornographic video in which Gerry featured prominently. Was it possible Alan had found it?

"Only he was on the news this afternoon too."

So that was it. Alan hadn't been snooping round after all, and even if he had, he couldn't possibly have guessed the significance of his find. Come to that, Victor thought, it might just suit his own immediate purpose to show Alan the video now.

"Hang on a minute," he said. "I think I've got something in here that might interest you." And before Alan could say another word, he was on his way to the bedroom. "Why don't you pour us both another drink?"

Alan didn't need telling twice, and he was back in his seat with a full glass in his hand, by the time Victor reappeared in the doorway, chuckling.

"What are you looking so pleased about?" he said.

"You'll see," said Victor, picking up the video remote.

"Come on…what are you up to?" said Alan, but he had spotted the tape in Victor's hand, and already he could feel that old familiar tingling in his legs.

Victor said nothing, but inserted the film in the machine, switched it on, and then came and took his place on the floor at Alan's feet.

Still the game went on, and even as the reel took up the slack and the film began to whirr, Alan felt the need to say something; but his throat didn't seem to want to co-operate, and when he did manage to speak, it was hardly more than a whisper.

"What's this got to do with Gerry Swallows?" he said.

"You'll see," said Victor again, and they both fell silent.

The picture took a long time to settle, but when it did the scene was a familiar one, a group of men in shorts and vests, working out in a gymnasium. The camera scanned the room slowly, five muscular bodies hard at work, glistening with sweat. There was an unmarked door at one end of the gym, and through it a locker room, two showers unattended. One man finished his exercises, rubbed himself down with a towel, and ambled towards the door...another followed. Cut...

To an office, which gave one the impression of being connected to the gym, and two men in dinner suits standing over a semi-clad figure, who was clearly supposed to have been knocked out in training. Alan would have recognised Gerry Swallows anywhere. One of the men was slapping his face, while the other was busy removing his kit, and Gerry was slowly beginning to stir.

So were the folds of Alan's dressing gown, and this time, Victor was pleased to observe, there was unlikely to be any further delay.

Esther...

Esther had spent the last hour packing a bag to take to Denby Green with her...she wasn't sure when. But then she wasn't sure of anything any more...

The news of Tim's death had been broken to her three times now – by a newsreader on television last night, by the police shortly afterwards, and by her daughter-in-law, Heather, on the phone this morning – Heather, who had been alongside Tim in the swimming pool when the ambulance crew arrived at the Manor House. And the upshot of this morning's conversation had been that Esther should be ready to make her way to Denby Green at a moment's notice. Dave had gone out – to the pub, presumably – having told her she needed some time alone to grieve.

It was three months now since she'd married Dave, three weeks since she'd met Sylvia on Brighton seafront, and the enormity of her mistake had begun to crystallise.

"This is what I reckon," Sylvia had said, after hearing her story. "Dave knew Roger was looking for a property in your part of the world, so he kept his eyes open, and when he knocked on your door he saw an opportunity to do himself a bit of good as well. So he took you out for lunch, liked what he heard, and then put in an offer on your place himself – or got one of his pals to, in case you made the connection. Sat on it for a couple of weeks, knowing you weren't the type of woman to welsh on a deal, and then withdrew his offer before showing up a day later with Roger."

"You mean he planned the whole thing?" said Esther.

"No, I wouldn't go as far as that," said Sylvia. "Dave's a chancer, not a planner, but he knows a vulnerable woman when he sees one, and he gambled on the fact that in your fragile state you'd accept Roger's lower offer rather than have to start the process all over again. So he earned his commission, and your undying gratitude into the bargain, and…I'll bet it was him who put you on to Clive too, wasn't it?"

Clive Wolstenholme, who'd probably never seen a

donkey in his life, never mind moved to Madrid to save one.

"I feel sick," said Esther.

"Yes, well don't beat yourself up about it," said Sylvia. "You're not the first one, I can assure you."

Esther had spent the weeks since that conversation waiting for her solicitor to return from a month-long holiday, and guide her back to the dull but predictable world she had once shared with Oliver. Sylvia had offered to send in the boys if she liked – the boys being her nephew, Andy and his partner, Dan, who had booted Dave out of one house already, and were perfectly capable of doing it again. But Sylvia was still in dispute with Dave about a joint account that had been closed for months, if not years, and Esther had no intention of pursuing her association with Dave into the next century. Or at least she hadn't until last night. Now she couldn't care less.

She left her suitcase in her bedroom, and made her way to the kitchen, where she found Ben lying on the floor, looking pleased with himself, and surrounded by the shredded pages of a magazine he had just torn to pieces. She got down on her knees to start clearing it up, and found herself staring at the fragmented image of a naked woman being raped for the amusement of a group of men in uniform.

Dave...

Saturday night was the only time of the week when the antique boys were outnumbered by the rest of the punters at the Regent, which is why the landlord, Hugh, made it his business to look after them.

He knew it wouldn't last, because he'd seen it all before, in the Cock and Bottle, where he'd once been a regular himself, and the arrival in the saloon bar of a couple of strangers one evening had been enough of an event to provoke comment after they'd gone. The following day they'd come back with another man in tow, and by the end of the week they'd virtually taken the place over.

A pattern had soon developed, involving lock-ins every Friday night, gee-gees Saturday afternoons, wives and girlfriends Sunday lunchtime. The rest of the week was a bit more hit and miss, but there were always a few of them in there...mouthing, spending.

And then one blustery November afternoon – Newbury on the telly, and no excuse to be anywhere except propping up a bar – nothing. Not one of them had appeared all day – and they'd never come back. Now it was the Regent's turn.

They were a pretty noisy bunch, although they didn't shout about their business. Just the usual man stuff – sport, politics, women.

One or two of them had shops of their own – a clock specialist, a jeweller – but from what Hugh could gather, the rest made their living out of auctions and flea markets, boot sales and charity shops...knocking on doors ...charming their way into people's homes. Hugh didn't ask.

It was just starting to get busy when Dave Savage got up to go – a bit early for him for a Saturday night, but he didn't want to leave Esther on her own for too long.

That was what he told the others, anyway, having told them two hours earlier that he'd only come out at all to give her a bit of space.

"You're all heart," had been Roger's response then, but he held his tongue now, Hugh noticed, and not a bad judge either. That Dave could be a tricky bastard when he'd had a few.

Esther…

After finding the remains of Dave's magazine on the kitchen floor, Esther's behaviour was surprisingly composed for a woman who thought she was going out of her mind. And there was no doubt that it was Dave's. She'd traced it back to his bedroom, and a stash of a dozen or more in a leather briefcase on the floor of his wardrobe. No wonder he didn't want her in there.

She left the briefcase where she'd found it, and returned to the kitchen, where she swept up every scrap of the torn magazine, and stuffed it into one of the spare carrier bags she kept hanging on a hook behind the cellar door. Then she put Ben on his lead, collected the suitcase she'd packed earlier from her room, and walked out of the house.

It took her half an hour or so to find a bin, where she could dump the evidence without being seen. After that she flagged down a taxi, and gave the driver Sylvia's address.

Trish, Louise…

Trish and Louise were drinking whisky now. The coffee cups had been put away more than an hour ago, as had any ideas Trish may have had about a game of cards; and the conversation, such as it was, was across the hearth now, rather than the kitchen table.

Back there they had agreed to shelve Louise's plans for an affair until tomorrow, and having done so had arrived at a moment of anti-climax, during which each of them had returned in her thoughts to Tim. The move to the living room had intervened, and since then the conversation had become more reflective, punctuated as it was by silences which grew longer and longer. It was Louise who was the more troubled of the two.

"Don't you ever wonder what's the point of it all?" she said. "I mean, look at me, for God's sake – seventy years of age, and still chasing round the place looking for a way of holding on to some old fool I should probably have let go years ago. And for what? I might be dead tomorrow."

"I know," said Trish. "But it's no good trying to look for answers at a time like this, because you always come back to Tim in the end."

"Mmm…it's an interesting thought though, isn't it, that we might behave differently if we knew when it was all going to end? I mean, what would you do if you were told you were going to die tomorrow?"

"I don't know. Put a couple of bottles of champagne in the fridge, I should think. Why, what would you do?"

Louise thought about Max, and what she would be prepared to go through to be with him at the end. A twelve-hour flight to L.A.? A long drive from the airport? How many hours would that leave?

"Not enough," she said. "I mean, I don't think a day

would be enough time for me to do what I wanted to do. What about a week?"

Trish laughed.

"It was you who made the rules," she said. "And anyway, a week might not be enough, if that was all you were given."

Louise frowned.

"That's a funny word to use," she said. "The word 'given', I mean. It implies some sort of divine hand at work."

"Not to me, it doesn't," said Trish. "Why, what's that husband of yours been saying now?"

"No, it's nothing to do with Max. I was just thinking about this article I was reading on the plane, that's all…about death, and what it means to people of different cultures. You've heard of karma, haven't you?"

"Yes, of course. Just remind me what it is again."

"Well, according to this article, it's the Buddhist equivalent of reaping what you sow. Only they believe in reincarnation, you see, so your karma is there to ensure that everything you do in this life is taken into account in the next."

"A bit like heaven and hell, really?"

"Yes, except I think people would be far more likely to behave themselves if they thought they were going to suffer the consequences of their actions back here, rather than in some place they can't even begin to imagine. Not that I'm thinking of becoming a Buddhist or anything. I just think it's a good philosophy to live by, that's all."

"I couldn't agree more. Do as you would be done by, sort of thing."

"Yes."

"Or come back as an ant."

But Louise wasn't in the mood for jokes.

"It makes sense, though, doesn't it?" she said. "You know, given the unforgivable things some people get away with in this life, it does only seem fair that they should pay for them in the next."

"I'm not sure fairness comes into it," said Trish. "Still, if that's what gives you peace of mind…"

Peace of mind – one of the few luxuries life had never thrown Louise's way, feeling guilty as she did for having so much more than she deserved, in a world where so many people had so much less; while the likes of Trish seemed to be able to accept their own good fortune without a qualm. Unlike her brother and sister, Trish had always been comfortable in her own skin. Louise could see them now, the three of them as children…

Trundling around East Anglia in a caravan with their parents, who ran a small travelling theatre company. In a world full of poverty and cruelty and prejudice, she was already beginning to question her own place in it. But it was no good talking to Trish even then.

Yes, the world was a rotten place, she would say in her offhand way – always had been, always would be – so the least anyone in her position could do was to make the most of her own good fortune, and live a happy life. There certainly wasn't any point in everyone being miserable…was there? It was a cosy philosophy, if only you could stomach it.

And then there was Oliver. The third child of three, Oliver had been a troubled child, until he found God's love and Esther, and saw no need to look any further. It wasn't fair.

All three of them had started acting before they could walk – no one ever nursed a doll in one of Reg and Tilly Court's productions – but Oliver never caught the bug, and it would be the two girls who brought the family name to worldwide attention.

Trish was the first one to leave the fold. She received a letter from Blatch Robinson, inviting her over to New York for a holiday, and offering to pay her fare. Blatch was a former member of the company, who had sailed to the States a few months after the end of the war, to look for the GI who had talked about marrying her. That hadn't worked out, but she had followed up one or two contacts while she was there, and now her career was beginning to take off, so…

Trish accepted her invitation, and what had been intended as a three-week break, turned into a successful stage and film career, which was to keep her away from England for years.

Louise was the next to go. Again it was supposed to be a holiday – in Beverly Hills this time rather than New York, and at Trish's invitation rather than Blatch's – but there was more to it than that.

One of the big film studios had acquired the rights to an unknown novel by an unheard of writer, which just so happened to have become the blockbuster of its year; and now they were rushing to cast the movie, which was being hyped as the major event of the decade.

The story was a romance, set against a background of the American Civil War, and the studio had no trouble finding the right man to play the lead. There was no shortage of candidates for the female lead either – in fact they were tripping over each other in the rush – but it was an unusual part. The heroine wasn't a heroine in the normal sense of the word. She was a prostitute, an opportunist with a sharp figure and an even sharper tongue, taking advantage of the country's youth, poor little soldier boys, who knew no better, and in less unfortunate times would have been back home playing with toy guns and marrying their childhood sweethearts. Her romance was to be with one of these boys, who would fight and win many a courageous battle, before ditching her for an innocent general's daughter.

The studio heads were cautious – nobody seemed quite right for the part somehow – and although they talked of short-lists and so on, it was almost as if they were afraid of making a decision.

It was round about this time that Trish had her greatest moment of inspiration. She was a star by now, and she was available too, so naturally she'd familiarised herself with the character as best she could. But she was realistic too. It wasn't for her, this part. However, even before she dared to form her plan, in trying to picture the heroine of the story, it was always Louise she saw in the hero's arms. She had no idea why. It just was.

She didn't tell a soul, but instead sent Louise an invitation to come and visit, and organised a lavish party, so that her little sister could see at first hand the sort of wonderful life she was leading in Hollywood.

She made sure all the right people would be there, of course – in other words the right men, because in those days all the right people were men – and when they came, and she saw a group of them talking frenziedly in a corner – each looking round at Louise every few seconds in case she should disappear before his audacious plan could be put to her – she knew her gamble had paid off. The following day Louise was signed up.

The film was an enormous flop, but it gained notoriety as one of the most expensive turkeys ever made, and eventually achieved cult status on both sides of the Atlantic. But, more to the point, it brought Louise to the public's attention, and cast her in a mould she would never manage to break.

"A good contract's worth any number of good scripts," Victor Andrews had said to her once, many years later, and she'd despised him for it, partly because she always despised people who over-estimated their own cleverness, and partly because it had been a careless remark on her part that had caused him to say it.

She had been talking about her career – her sudden arrival in Hollywood, followed by years of being tied by contract to a studio that had a reputation for being the most tight-fisted of them all – and naturally for him, Victor had understood her preoccupation to be with the money she might have earned rather than the lousy parts she had been required to play, which were what she really regretted.

Later on – after her contract had expired – Louise had landed several worthwhile roles, which – amongst the general acclaim – had won her no less than three Oscar nominations and one precious statuette; but standards change, and even the best of her achievements looked outdated now, when she saw them on television. As for the rest…well…the less said about them the better.

Her father had said something to her once, which she had never forgotten. Had she been in a less receptive mood at the time, she may have been a different woman today. Had Reg Court known how deeply his words would still be affecting his daughter more than fifty years later, he might never have said them.

They'd been talking about fairness – or rather the lack of it – in a world where a girl seemed destined to a life of playing second fiddle to a less talented sister, just because she happened to be two years younger than her. This was not only an uncharacteristically spiteful thing to say, it was also untrue, and old Reg had no intention of letting it pass.

"In this life, young lady," he said, "you get what you deserve…"

It was exactly what Louise would have expected him to say – so much so that she could have laughed – would have done, if he'd left it at that. But it was an uncharacteristic moment all round, and he went on:

"…At least you'll get all the bad you deserve."

Then in a softer voice he added:

"All I can ask of you, is that you deserve all the good."

Now, by the fireside, Louise wondered just what she did deserve – surely a little peace of mind wouldn't be too much to ask? Funnily enough, the article she'd read on the plane home had claimed that it was that very phrase that lay at the heart of the Buddhist culture – peace of mind. What a wonderful thought. And then there was karma, which Trish had managed to distil into 'coming back as an ant'.

'If you wish to know of your past life, look to your present circumstances; if you wish to know of your future life, look to your present actions.' That was how the Buddhists put it apparently. But wasn't that the same as saying that Tim had deserved to be drowned?

No, Trish was absolutely right about one thing. It was no good trying to look for answers at a time like this, because you always came back to Tim in the end.

Sunday, 19

22 St Andrews Road
London N.5

1st September, 1944

Dearest Harold,

I hope you had a good birthday. With a bit of luck we shall all be together for the next one. But in the meantime, I want to tell you a story.

    When I was a girl my brother, Reg, was at school with a boy called Robert Cantwell, whose father was a master there, and kept a parrot in his study. Robert loved it, and when there was nothing else to do, he would sometimes spend his breaks trying to teach it to talk.

30 August 1944. It's Harold's thirteenth birthday, and one of the neighbours has baked him a cake, but when he's tempted to complain about the unfair way Aunt Violet is

sharing it out, he thinks better of it, and settles for what's put in front of him. It's more than he deserves – that's what she'd say – in fact he's lucky to have a cake at all in the circumstances.

The circumstances are that he was adopted seven years ago – by George and Celia Rathbone, who rescued him from the orphanage he'd lived in since his parents died. George and Celia already had two children of their own – John and Sissie – but they wanted a third, and they picked Harold because they were moved by his story. So he was lucky there too, according to Aunt Violet – lucky to have been in the right place at the right time – and everyone thought the Rathbones were saints for taking him on.

One of his teachers had put it another way, dangling a piece of paper under his nose as evidence:

"Don't you think your parents deserve better than this, after all the sacrifices they've made for you?"

He forgets the particular piece of work that prompted that remark, but he has never forgotten the remark itself, although he couldn't have been more than seven at the time.

On the other hand, he also remembers an occasion when one of his paintings was selected to be pinned up on the classroom wall. He was so proud of himself, he could hardly wait to tell the family about it; and then immediately regretted it when Ma said how pleased she was, and he saw the look of resentment in his brother's eyes. Another lesson learnt.

Then in 1939 he was evacuated to Devon, along with John and Sissie, whose Aunt Violet lived in Brixham, and the enthusiasm with which she greeted the two of them was so overdone, Harold wondered if it was calculated to make him feel unwelcome.

It was. As far as Violet was concerned family meant blood, and she was going to do everything she could to undermine Harold's claim on hers.

Five years on, and it was the same story all over again. John and Sissie were made as welcome as ever, but Violet begrudged Harold every minute he spent at her table…and she didn't mind who knew it. When he cleared his plate he was greedy; when he didn't he was ungrateful…

But he was neither of those things, which is why he never complained; and on his thirteenth birthday, he settled for the smallest piece of cake Aunt Violet could cut…while John and Sissie sat by pretending not to notice…

Three days later he received a letter.

22 St Andrews Road
London N.5

1st September, 1944

Dearest Harold,

I hope you had a good birthday. With a bit of luck we shall all be together for the next one. But in the meantime, I want to tell you a story.

When I was a girl my brother, Reg, was at school with a boy called Robert Cantwell, whose father was a master there, and kept a parrot in his study. Robert loved it, and when there was nothing else to do, he would sometimes spend his breaks trying to teach it to talk.

Our mother had died unexpectedly just a few days before Reg was due to start school, which meant it was halfway through the Christmas term by the time he arrived, and he had no idea that the parrot even existed. Mr. Cantwell volunteered to meet Reg at the station, and took Robert with him to help break the ice. On the way back they stopped at a teashop, where there was a canary singing in a cage above the counter. Seeing Reg looking at it, Mr. Cantwell asked him if he had any pets of his own, and Reg said, yes, he had a dog, but that our father had always taught us it was wrong to try and domesticate wild animals.

Mr. Cantwell pointed out that dogs were once wild too, and Reg agreed, but said that that was a long time ago, and dogs couldn't fly, could they? No one asked Robert what he thought.

A few days later Reg was summoned to Mr. Cantwell's study, where he saw the parrot for the first time, and the implication of what he had said in the teashop sunk in. But before he could make amends, Mr. Cantwell stopped him, and said he agreed with him. It was cruel to keep birds caged up, but the parrot's previous owner had been an old friend of his, who had died suddenly, so he felt honour-bound to look after it, and to let it go would be to sentence it to death.

Reg was not so sure about that, but said that whether it was true or not, if he was a parrot he would rather take his chances. At that moment Robert walked *in, and something about his manner made Reg wonder if he had been listening at the door.*

The next morning the housekeeper found the parrot's cage empty, and Mr. Cantwell's study window open. No sign of the parrot, until half an hour later, when it was found dead on the lawn outside the headmaster's window.

The Head broke the news at assembly, and when he did, Reg thought he could see a look of triumph on Robert's face, but it soon vanished when Mr. Cantwell interrupted the proceedings to announce that he had let the parrot out of its cage himself, and he must have left the window open by mistake.

Reg was sure he was lying, and years later, when he and Mr. Cantwell had become good friends, Mr. Cantwell admitted it. But he refused to say what had actually happened. Refused to betray his son, was how Reg put it to me when he told me about it afterwards – and that was fine by him.

You would like Reg. In fact, when this terrible war is over, I am going to take you to meet him and his family. Just the two of us. Better not mention it to John and Sissie. It can be our little secret.

> *Your loving,*
> *Ma*

It's early morning, and Harold is lying on his bunk at Calumet, reading Ma's letter for the last time. More than fifty years have gone by since the day he received it, and he still doesn't know what prompted Ma to send it; but he understands its meaning, and he's as impressed by it today as he was at the time – by its honesty, and the fact that it doesn't promise what it can't deliver. This is how we stand, Ma is saying. I know my children are in the wrong, and I'll do everything I can to put things right; but don't force me to take sides, because if I had to choose, I'd choose them.

Blood again, but unlike Aunt Violet, Ma had love to spare, and the paragraph that Harold always dwells on longest is the one in which she promised to take him to meet Reg and his family.

The best thing that had ever happened to him – that was what he thought at the time – but if he'd been able to see into the future back then, would he have chosen to go?

Esther, Sylvia, Andy, Dan...

At nine o' clock every Sunday morning, Sylvia woke Andy and Dan with a cup of tea, and then sat on the end of their bed chatting to them, while they drank it. But her knock on the door was lighter this morning, and her voice not much more than a whisper when she said:

"Esther's here."

It was three weeks now since Esther had come into their lives, and knowing what Sylvia had been through with Dave, 'the boys' had been more than willing to throw him out of her place too, but she'd turned them down, and settled for their friendship instead.

A couple of days later, Dan was reading an article in one of the Sunday supplements – about theatrical dynasties past and present – when he came across an interview with Patricia Court.

"My grandfather was a wealthy industrialist," she said…

> And when my father was a boy, he used to entertain him with stories about his underprivileged childhood, and the fair that used to visit his home town every spring. There were boxing booths, freak shows – that sort of thing – and a travelling theatre, which used to arrive in a convoy of horse-drawn caravans, and leave in the same way a week or so after the rest had gone. My father was always fascinated by the idea of taking the theatre to the audience rather than the other way round, so when Grandpa died he used his share of his fortune to set up a company of his own.
>
> By coincidence, his old school friend, Toby Allingham had just inherited the family title and the crippling death duties on the estate that went with it, so Dad killed two birds with one stone, and bought a nice chunk of land off him, with four workers' cottages, a paddock and some stables, and that was where they were based for the next twenty-odd years…actors, caravans, horses – the lot. I was born there, and I stayed until 1947, when an ex-member of the company invited me to New York, and then Louise followed me three years later. My brother, Oliver wasn't very interested in theatre, so when Dad died, he and his wife, Esther…

And so it went on. There was a photograph of them all at the bottom of the page – Trish, Louise, Oliver, Esther…and Harold Masters – fooling around in front of a caravan, with a horse grazing in the background. The picture was very old and grainy, but there was no mistaking anybody in it, and that was how Dan discovered that Esther was Timothy Court's mother. It was also why he and Sylvia and Andy had been watching *Shotgunning* on Friday night, when the news of Timothy's death was announced.

Now Esther was asleep in the room next door, her dog curled up by the side of the bed…or that was what Sylvia thought. But it was nine o'clock, which meant that Esther had been out for half an hour already – walking Ben around the park behind the house.

She was thinking about Harold, who would have heard the news by now, despite his determined attempts to keep the world at bay. Cassie would have told him…

Dear misguided Cassie, who had never been able to disguise the fact that she thought there was something going on between Harold and Esther, despite the lack of opportunity.

Esther couldn't remember the last time she'd been alone with Harold, but she'd allowed Cassie to go on believing the impossible – because it made her happy. Until one day Oliver's health took a turn for the worse, and it occurred to Esther that Cassie might think she and Harold were playing a waiting game; so she stopped going to Calumet, and used Oliver's illness as an excuse.

When Oliver died, Harold sent flowers, which she acknowledged with a promise to be in touch again soon, but it was months before she felt up to it, and when she did, Tim was away in France filming. She didn't dare visit Calumet without him, in case Cassie thought she was making her move. So she waited…until one day there was a knock on her door, and for a moment she was tempted to believe the impossible herself. But it wasn't Harold she found waiting on her step. It was Dave.

What a fool, she thought now, to have behaved so guiltily, when there was nothing to feel guilty about. The same could not be said of her relationship with Dave, but what did that matter? What did any of it matter any more? And then, with a rueful smile at her unfamiliar surroundings…apart from Ben's routine, of course.

Heather, Gerry…

Gerry had stayed the night again, and now he and Heather were at the dining room table enjoying a late breakfast.

"Are you really intending to go ahead with it?" he said. "This daffodil business, I mean?"

"Yes, of course," said Heather. "Why? Don't you think I should?"

"I don't see why not…if you think you can get away with it."

"It's not a question of getting away with anything. It's what Tim would have wanted, isn't it? Oh, and, before you ask, I'm sticking with the dress code too. No mourning…bright colours only…"

"Nice one. It'll give me a chance to show off my new linen suit. Have you told Esther yet?"

"Yes, she phoned while you were in the shower."

"What did she say?"

"What could she say? She's hardly going to deny her son his last wish, is she? Anyway, Tuesday's looking good if I can get everything arranged in time. Detective Inspector

Whatsisname phoned too, and he doesn't seem to think it'll be a problem. There'll have to be an inquest, apparently, but there's some sort of preliminary hearing tomorrow, so he's going to have a word with the coroner, and with a bit of luck he'll release the body for burial the following day."

"Oh, the body, yes," said Gerry, with a grin. "What did it used to be called again?"

Trish, Louise…

Ten-thirty on Sunday morning, and Louise was still in bed, while Trish was back at the kitchen table, drinking tea and listening to the omnibus edition of *The Archers* on the radio. It was something she was slightly ashamed to admit to – listening to *The Archers* – and yet she spent more time with the inhabitants of Ambridge than she did with anyone else.

There were one or two characters who didn't exist at all – not even in the second-hand way most radio characters do. They were spoken about – or even occasionally to – but in all the years Trish had been listening they had never said a word themselves, which made them nothing more than figments of a collective imagination; and yet one had died recently, and Trish had found herself in tears over it. Mad! Was that the telephone ringing?

Ten minutes later, *The Archers* forgotten, she was waking Louise with a cup of coffee.

"Esther's just been on the phone," she said, once Louise was wide enough awake to take in the news. "And all being well the funeral's on Tuesday."

"What do you mean, all being well?"

"Well, apparently they've got to clear it with the coroner first…But listen, that's not the interesting bit. It turns out that Tim's favourite flowers were daffodils…"

"Handy, at this time of year."

"Well, it is actually, yes, because according to Esther – who got it from Heather – it was Tim's express wish that there shouldn't be any other flowers at his funeral at all – only daffodils."

"Strange. I've never heard of anything like that before."

"No, neither have I. But you haven't heard the half of it yet…"

Belinda, Rodney…

There was nothing Belinda liked more than a Sunday at home with Rodney – in fact, when she was alone with him, and away from the temptations of everyday life, she often thought she'd be happier if she never had to go out again. It was when she went out that she took risks – with Jack, for instance, night after night in his friend Nobby's flat – and never mind the fact that Rodney might be checking her alibi as she betrayed him. She didn't seem to be able to stop herself. But how long could it go on before she was found out?

She had only got away with it so far because, for all his suspicions, Rodney wanted more than anything to be proved wrong, and she had learned how to protest her innocence so effectively, it was always he who ended up apologising to her in the end – for not trusting her in the first place. Oh well, only a couple of weeks to go now, and then, fond as she had become of Jack, it would be curtains for him, and another stab at fidelity.

The play they were touring together was the first work for the stage by a mildly controversial feminist novelist called Olivia Nuttall. It was a two-hander called *A Czech in the Post*, a woman's perspective on the history of the world and the men who have ruled it. Belinda and Jack had premiered it at Edinburgh last year.

One newspaper reviewer had commented:

'Ms Nuttall clearly doesn't believe in research, but simply taps into the latest current of popular opinion – however ill-informed – and makes it her own.'

But Ms Nuttall was an early riser, and before most people had had a chance to read the item in question, she had been on *The Today Programme* pointing out that her latest novel had just been serialised in the very same paper the review had appeared in. Surely that was tantamount to the editor calling his own readership ill-informed?

She had a point – it was popularly held – and *A Czech in the Post* had gone on to be one of the hits of the festival. The current tour was in its second month now, and was due to finish in Eastbourne the week after next.

From the security of Rodney's arms, that looked like a good time for Belinda to make a fresh start.

Victor, Simon, Alan…

There was an understanding between Victor and Simon, which must have been voiced some time long ago, although neither of them was aware of it, that Simon could arrive on Victor's doorstep at any time, day or night, and expect to find a welcome there.

Their story was one which would have struck a chord with Alan, in that they'd met at a badminton club, when Simon was a fifth-former and Victor was still light enough on his feet to get around the court.

In those days Simon was accustomed to the sort of attention he envied Alan now, and in Victor he immediately recognised all the signs of an impending approach. But when it came – on the first occasion they found themselves alone together in the changing rooms – it was Simon's friend, Neil, Victor asked about first.

"Is your friend not with you today?"

Nothing ever came of Victor's interest in Neil, not even when Simon was persuaded to invite him round to Victor's flat one day after school. The boy quickly become nervous and wanted to leave, but it was only when it fell to Simon to convince him that it would not be a good idea to mention their visit to anyone else – or the pictures Victor had shown them – that the truth dawned on him. Victor had been using him all along.

An unlikely beginning for a lasting friendship, but that was what Victor and Simon's relationship had become, and now there was always a welcome for Simon at Victor's door. In fact he had his own key.

"Hello? Anybody in?"

Victor came into the hall.

"Simon! What are you doing here?"

"I'll give you three guesses," said Simon, walking straight past Victor, and into the living room. "I'm not interrupting anything, am I?"

Victor smiled.

"He's gone down the road for some tonics."

"Oh, so he is still here then?" said Simon, poking his nose into the bedroom. "Good. I enjoyed myself the other night."

"Did you?"

"Yes, I did. Disappointed?"

"Why should I be disappointed?"

"No particular reason. Funny you didn't tell me you were going to be there, though."

"I thought I did."

"Liar…" And then throwing himself into his usual armchair: "…Anyway, never mind that now. I've got something to tell you."

"What about?" said Victor, lowering himself on to the settee.

"Ronnie…you'll never guess what he tried to tell me over dinner last night."

"Go on."

"Only that he'd had an affair with Tim Court, that's all."

"What?"

"Yeh…fucking rat! I threw my plate at him actually."

"Why? You don't believe him, do you?"

"No, of course not. Still hurt, though."

There was a buzz on the intercom, and Victor got up to answer it, saying:

"You know what your trouble is, don't you?"

"No," said Simon. "What?"

"You lack self-esteem."

"Oh yeh…you been reading *Woman's Own* again?"

"It's true," said Victor. "I mean what other grounds could

there possibly be for living with someone who wears a toupee?"

So he was joking – or that was what Simon tried to persuade himself while Victor was off answering the door – but the truth was that, funny or not, the question did still remain as to what Simon was doing living with a man like Ronnie. A rat in a toupee. Actually Ronnie didn't wear a toupee, but his immaculately coiffed hair was as black as a raven's wing, more or less as described on the label he was always careful to peel off the bottle he kept in the bathroom cabinet, and his teeth had been capped long ago by a prominent dentist who liked his work to be noticed. So what was Simon still doing with him?

Was it pity? Despite his contempt for Ronnie – or perhaps because of it – Simon couldn't help feeling sorry for the man. Maybe it was gratitude? Life with Ronnie had provided him with certain material advantages after all. Or was it love? The truth was that Ronnie had never been able to resist the temptation to brag, and even in the anonymous bedsit he had once kept solely for the purpose of entertaining the likes of Simon, he had often proved incapable of keeping his good connections to himself. When Simon's turn had come, he had been quick to recognise the name Delaney as one that might be useful to him, but slow to realise that it never would. Ten years on, and he was on the brink of success at last, although no thanks to Ronnie or his connections, but now that he could afford to leave, to do so would be to admit that the last ten years had been nothing more than a waste of time, the best ten years of his life sacrificed for something he could have achieved anyway. No, it was too much to ask of himself. Perhaps it was love after all. Ronnie would have said so anyway.

Alan followed Victor into the living room, saying:

"Sorry I was so long. They only had slimline in the place round the corner, so I…oh…hello…"

"Hi," said Simon, but before another word could be spoken the telephone started ringing, and Victor disappeared into the bedroom with the portable handset, only to reappear in the doorway a few seconds later to mouth the word 'Heather' at them, before disappearing again and shutting the door.

"So…" said Simon, with a smile that Alan found impossible to decipher. "Still here, then?"

"Yes. I'm not due back till Thursday."

"Back where?"

"Carlisle."

"Oh…right."

"In Cumbria."

Simon smiled again, and Alan said:

"We're going for a drink this lunchtime. Why don't you come with us?"

"Sounds good…" A long pause, and then Simon said: "Have you known Vic long?"

"No, only a few days. Some lad on the coach down told me about this pub near Leicester Square. I forget what it was called now."

"The Bear and Whippet, probably."

"Yeh, that's it. I bumped into Vic on the way there."

"Easily done. Is this your first time in London then?"

"Mmm…my Mum thinks I'm in the Lakes with my mates."

"You're joking…?"

"No…she doesn't know I'm gay, you see."

"And what do you think would happen if she found out?"

"I don't know…"

Simon was not so naïve as to believe he knew the answer to that question either, although it had often struck him how unjust it was that so many gay people felt it incumbent upon themselves to live a lie, not simply because of the daily threats they would face if they did come clean – like ridicule and discrimination and actual bodily harm and so on – but because they didn't want to inconvenience their family and friends.

Alan said:

"Do you know anything about born-again Christians?"

"Not really, no…why?"

"Because my mum's one, and now she's got it into her head that you have to be a believer to stand a chance of getting to Heaven."

"Sorry, but is this still to do with her not knowing you're gay?"

"It is, yeh…you see, a couple of weeks ago I heard Vinnie – that's her boyfriend – telling her about these two guys, who had to leave the church because they were in a sexual relationship."

"You mean they were kicked out?"

"No, no…they decided to leave themselves, because they couldn't accept that what they were doing was a sin."

"Well, good for them."

"I know. But I'm pretty sure Vinnie would have

preferred to kick them out, because the way he told it, it was as if he'd been cheated…and then he saw me looking at him, and he tried to make out he hadn't meant it like that at all."

"Do you think he knows, then?"

"What, about me being gay, you mean? No, he's not interested enough to know anything about me. He just didn't like being caught out, that's all. Prick…"

"Doesn't sound to me as if you're very keen on Vinnie."

"I'm not. But I can't say anything, because…you know…I don't want to upset my mum."

Ringing for a taxi a few minutes later, Victor was surprised at how little interest Simon and Alan had taken in the news that Heather had asked him to make the arrangements for Tim's funeral.

"Still, you don't keep a dog and bark yourself," he'd said, by way of explaining how he'd passed the job on to one of his underlings, but they hadn't seemed particularly impressed by that either. Never mind. He hadn't got to the best bit yet.

Simon said:

"Victor knows a bit about Christianity, don't you, Victor?"

"Do I?" he said, and then into the telephone: "Oh, hello, I thought you'd all gone home. May I have a cab, please, to the penthouse flat, number one Canterbury Court…yes, straight away."

Trish, Louise…

Trish and Louise were taking their time over lunch, and

the subject under discussion was immortality. It had started naturally enough with Louise wondering aloud how well, and how long, and for what, Tim would be remembered. They had turned it into a game of sorts, searching through history for immortals.

The Bible had come first, but neither of them were great readers of The Bible, and they couldn't be sure whether the characters that sprung to mind had ever really existed. Adam and Eve? There was Jesus Christ of course. Well, he was a good one to start with. Next came Boadicea – Boadicea and Julius Caesar – but all they knew about them was that Boadicea was a queen who rode round on a chariot, and Julius Caesar had had a play written about him by Shakespeare. William Shakespeare. Now there was an immortal if ever there was one. Both Louise and Trish felt quite smug to have thought of him, and proud to have spoken his name, both being more closely associated with him through their art, so to speak – and yet neither of them had performed a single line of Shakespeare since their days with their father's travelling theatre, and if you'd asked Louise how many plays he'd written, her spontaneous answer would have been 'seven'.

Having taken an enormous leap forward in history, they retreated a century or two – albeit unknowingly – to Joan of Arc.

"What did she do again?"

"She got burnt at the stake, I know that much."

Next came Mozart, but they agreed not to bring up any more composers or the game could go on forever. Rembrandt brought down the same fate upon artists, and Charles Dickens on novelists. Napoleon got a mention.

Trish knew quite a lot about him, and she rounded off his story by mentioning his defeat by Wellington, his banishment to St Helena, and the fact that she was sure he had invented decimals. Nelson was an admiral who had played a trick by putting a telescope to his blind eye, and apart from a smattering of kings and queens and Guy Fawkes, that brought them to the twentieth century.

They picked them at random. Queen Victoria at the end of a long reign; Einstein, for his Theory of Relativity, whatever that was. Then there was Hitler. Neither of them wanted to count him, but they had to admit he couldn't be ignored. Stalin? Well, grudgingly. Gandhi? Ah, yes. John F. Kennedy? Nobody would ever forget where they were the day he died. Louise remembered Martin Luther King.

"He was assassinated too, wasn't he?" said Trish.

"Yes, but I remember him for that marvellous speech he made that time. 'I have a dream,' he kept saying. Do you remember?"

"I remember the phrase, yes, although I must confess I didn't know it was him."

"God, we're an ignorant pair when you think about it, aren't we?"

Trish laughed.

"Oh, I don't suppose we're any worse than anyone else," she said. "And anyway, we haven't come to the people in our own field yet, have we?"

"No, true…Clark Gable then."

"What…immortal?"

"Yes. I'm afraid oral hygiene doesn't come into it. Go on. Your turn."

"All right then…Vincente Rossi."

"Oh yes," said Louise, before adding: "Does he count though? I thought you had to be dead to qualify."

"I don't see why," said Trish. "And anyway, he is dead, isn't he?"

"He's not, is he?"

"I think so, yes. Or am I getting him mixed up with someone else? Do you know, I can't honestly remember."

"Neither can I. Isn't it terrible?"

Trish thought it was funny.

"So much for immortality," she said. "Actually though, it doesn't make the slightest bit of difference when you think about it, does it? Dead or alive, we still think as much of him, so as far as we're concerned, I suppose he really is immortal."

But Louise wasn't so sure. This was a subject close to her heart, and if she and her sister could be so offhand about the fate of the greatest director who ever lived, what chance was there for her, with very little but a string of outdated films and unremarkable husbands to her credit? Perhaps there was still time.

"I wonder," she said, thinking about time and the lack of it. "I wonder if Timothy will go down in history as one of the all time greats…or do you think he was too young?"

"I don't know," said Trish. "Probably…probably too young, I mean."

"Mmm…"

There was a slight pause and then Louise said:

"Perhaps he'll become a cult figure."

"You make it sound as if he had a choice," said Trish, but the wicked glint she was half expecting to see in her sister's eye was not there, and she went on more thoughtfully:

"Mind you, I wouldn't be surprised if he did. You only have to die an unexpected death these days, and you're halfway there, aren't you? I just hope for Esther's sake the media don't try and make more of him than there was."

"What do you mean?"

"Well, there's not enough meat on a story like Tim's, is there? Before you know where you are they'll have him snorting cocaine and sleeping three in a bed…gambling away the family fortune…"

"No…do you think so?"

"Well I wouldn't be surprised. And I'll tell you another thing. Turning his funeral into a carnival isn't going to help matters."

Simon, Victor, Alan…

"Talking about self-esteem…" said Simon.

"Which we weren't," said Victor, in whose opinion both of his companions had had far too much to say for themselves during the past hour.

"Oh, I think we were, Victor…"

They were sitting at a table now, in a quiet corner of one of Victor's favourite pubs, and he'd just come back from the bar with a tray of drinks.

"Did you know Vic went to boarding school?" Simon said to Alan.

"No?" said Alan.

"Oh yes," said Simon. "And he had this arrangement with one of the Christian Brothers who ran it."

"What sort of arrangement?"

"He used to suck him off after lessons…only the Brothers didn't approve of that sort of thing, and Vic's friend always used to feel guilty once he'd shot his load, so to square it with his conscience he used to beat the shit out of Vic afterwards for tempting him in the first place."

"Why didn't you report him?" said Alan, once Victor had confirmed Simon's story.

"Who to?" said Victor. "Do you really think they would have taken my word against his?"

"They would now," said Simon.

"Oh yes, they probably would now – whether I was telling the truth or not – but it was different in those days. And besides, in some ways it suited me to keep things the way they were."

"How come?" said Alan.

"Well, I was grateful, I suppose. I'd always been bullied until he came along, you see. In fact, I think it was the victim in me that appealed to him in the first place."

"I'm sure it was," said Simon.

"Oh, I don't think he really meant to hurt me, Simon," said Victor. "You said it yourself, it was just guilt, and anyway, he did manage to put a stop to the bullying, so at least after that I knew where my punishment was coming from."

"Your punishment?" said Alan.

"Like putting all your debts on one credit card," said Simon. "You may not be any better off, but at least you know where you stand."

"Yes, well we all know how you feel about it, Simon," said Victor. "But it was a very long time ago…and anyway, it must have done me some good, mustn't it, because nobody's ever tried to bully me since."

"And that makes what he did right, does it?"

"No, of course not. But nor does it make Christian teaching wrong, if that's what you're trying to say."

"Which is why you were at Mass at eight o'clock this morning."

"Simon, what is it you're asking me to apologise for?"

"I'm not. It just makes me sick, that's all."

"Yes, well…"

"I don't suppose you heard what Alan was saying about his mother before, did you?"

"No…what?"

"She's a born-again Christian…which means that in her book the likes of us are destined for eternal damnation."

"So what's new? A lot of people in my own church believe the same thing…"

"Aah, but my mum doesn't just believe it," said Alan. "She knows."

Trish, Louise…

Two hours had gone by since lunch, most of which Trish had spent dozing in her favourite armchair. Louise was trying to read, but she kept finding herself staring into the distance, lost in thought. Then she would look across at Trish hopefully, but she'd never had the heart to disturb a peaceful sleep, so back to her book she would go…and the cycle would start again.

When Trish did eventually wake up, Louise slapped the

open book face down on the table beside her, and said:

"At last! If I've read that page once I must have read it a hundred times."

"What's the matter?" said Trish, stretching her arms in preparation for a move. "You're not still thinking about Tim, are you?"

"I don't seem to be able to think about anything else," said Louise.

"I know," said Trish. "I'm the same."

They fell silent for a moment, as if to underline the fact that they were both thinking about him, and then Louise said:

"I wonder which would be worse? To be remembered for something awful…or…or untrue…or not to be remembered at all?"

"Eh?" said Trish, and then remembering the conversation over lunch:

"We are still talking about Tim, are we?"

"Yes, of course," said Louise. "Who else?"

"Well then," said Trish. "You've obviously been giving the matter some thought. What do you think?"

"I think…" said Louise. "I think that if Tim had the choice, he would choose to be honourably forgotten."

"I think you're right," said Trish, and lifting herself slowly out of her chair, she went over and kissed Louise on the forehead.

"What was that for?" said Louise.

"Never mind…I'll go and put the kettle on, shall I?"

She was halfway to the kitchen, before Louise called her back.

"Trish?"

"Yes?" she said, popping her head round the door.

"I was just wondering," said Louise. "How does one go about getting oneself burnt at the stake?"

Heather, Gerry…

Heather was sitting at Tim's desk, going through a list she had drawn up earlier, of things that needed to be done in preparation for the funeral. Gerry was half-sitting, half-lying on the settee, watching her.

"I must say, you're taking all this very seriously," he said. " I don't think I've ever seen you at a desk before."

Pretending not to have heard, Heather put a line through the last item on the list, and then sat back, saying:

"Right then. That seems to be it for the moment. Let's just hope everything goes smoothly tomorrow, that's all."

"What, with the coroner, you mean?"

"Yes…oh, and by the way, I don't have to go. I spoke to Detective Inspector Whatsit again this afternoon, and he said there isn't any need, so I'm not. He's promised to phone and let me know what happens. I think he fancies me actually."

"I'm sure he does. What about the funeral?"

"Midday on Tuesday, all being well. I've asked Victor to deal with that side of things."

"Victor! Why?"

"Well, he probably knows the rules, doesn't he? I mean, I don't know. What do you do? Send out invitations, or something…? Or just phone people up?"

Gerry had to confess he didn't know either.

"Anyway," said Heather, "he's more than happy to do it. So…let's just hope World War Three doesn't break out in the meantime. We might even make a few front pages."

Cassie…

Cassie was lying on her bed, staring at a row of books on the shelf above her, and trying to focus on one in particular – *Beyond the Horizon*, by one of the founders of Calumet, Larry Duncan Campbell. The idea was that if she concentrated hard enough, she could make it fall off the shelf, and on to the bed beside her.

Chapter Three of *Beyond the Horizon* was devoted to the phenomenon known as telekinesis, and it was Cassie's romantic notion that the book would fall open in the middle of it: but the catch was that to make something happen, you had to believe in your ability to make it happen – and Cassie didn't. She was just killing time until Larry arrived. And when he did come, it would not be with the intention of discussing his book.

In fact it was only a recent conversation with Harold that had made her think of it in the first place – Harold, last seen sitting under his favourite tree in the top field. One day last week she had walked into his caravan to find him leafing through the pages of a book of quotations.

"What you looking up?" she said.

"Mountains," he said, and then reading from the page: "'*And though I have the gift of prophesy, and understand all mysteries, and all knowledge; and though I have all faith, so that I could remove mountains, and have not charity, I am nothing.*' Recognise it?"

"Yes, of course," said Cassie. "It's from Gabriel's sermon in the last scene of *Shotgunning*."

"Spot on," said Harold.

"So…what made you think of it?" said Cassie.

"Well, funnily enough, it was something Larry said in that book you lent me…about telekinesis, and the power of the mind and so on. He raised the question of where these powers come from. And that made me wonder. Where were *Gabriel's* powers supposed to have come from?"

"Does it matter?" said Cassie. "I mean, surely what matters is not where they came from, but what he did with them…bearing in mind what he could have been starting, I mean. You know what they say about a butterfly flapping its wings in Guatemala…?"

"Funny you should mention that," said Harold. "I remember thinking much the same thing when we were shooting the film."

"And what do you think now?"

"I think…" said Harold, getting up from the table. "I think it's time we had a glass of wine."

But if Cassie saw this as Harold's jokey way of trying to change the subject, she was wrong, because when he sat down again, he said:

"You could always start small, I suppose."

"What do you mean?" she said.

"Well…if you were afraid of what might happen. You could do something inconsequential like…like sitting under a tree, and willing a leaf to fall into your hand."

"Oh, I see," she said. "Yes…but what would be the point of that? Leaves fall off trees all the time, don't they? So you wouldn't be sure if it was you who'd made it happen."

"All right then," he said. "Let's think of something else."

"I know," she said, eyeing the bookshelf above his head. "We could concentrate on one of the books up there, and try and make *that* fall off."

But after about a minute she was forced to admit defeat.

"No, it's no good," she said. "I've got something I need to tell you."

"What?"

"Larry's asked me to go away with him."

Monday, 20

THE NORFOLK PLAYERS

present

Reginald Court   Matilda Court   Ian Maw
Blatch Robinson
Patricia Court   Louise Court
and
Harold Masters as Philip Pirrip

in

WOMEN & CHILDREN FIRST

by

Reginald Court

Ma was as good as her word, and in the summer of 1946 she managed to steal Harold away to Norfolk for a few days, having convinced John and Sissie what a dull time was in store for them if they decided to go too. On the train she said what a pity it was that they hadn't been able to come, and Harold was quick to agree, but he had a letter in his pocket about a schoolboy called Reg and an incident with a parrot…better not mention it…our little secret…

They lived in a cottage on the edge of a large country estate near the village of May – Uncle Reg and his wife, Tilly, their daughters, Trish and Louise, and their son, Oliver – and they were preparing to go on the road again after a six-year lay off, during which Reg had been winning the war single-handed, and Tilly had been helping out in the big house up the drive. But the season was half over already, and they were still so far behind with their preparations, Reg had been forced to compromise; and now they were planning a much shorter programme, to be performed locally for a couple of weeks in August, while working towards a full season starting next Easter. The Norfolk Players…

"What do you reckon, Tilly? Mister Copperfull or Dodger?"

It was the first thing Reg said after welcoming Harold into his home, and Harold didn't have a clue what he was talking about, although it did have a friendly ring to it…so friendly, in fact, that Harold couldn't help wondering if Reg's son might begrudge him the attention. But when he glanced in Oliver's direction, Oliver just rolled his eyes, as if to say:

"Take no notice. He's like this with everyone."

There was a cake for tea, which Tilly cut into eight pieces – one each all round, and one spare, which she shared between the boys when their plates were empty. No arguments, no resentful looks – no more-than-you-deserves at Tilly's table – and for the first time since he was led away from Aggie Jemison's burning house, Harold felt at home.

Later that night, when the rest of the family were in bed, and Ma and Reg were alone together in front of the fire, they talked seriously for the first time in nearly seven years, but the closest Reg came to discussing his war was to praise Tilly's part in getting him through it, and he soon brought the subject round to Ma's other reason for wanting to talk to him alone – Harold. So she started where she'd left off in 1939, and spared him no details, despite what it said about the way John and Sissie had behaved in Devon.

"Three times I sent him there, Reg – three times – and neither of them ever said a word about what went on."

"How did you find out?" said Reg.

"Oh, she told me herself," said Ma.

"Who, Violet?"

"Yes…the day after Harold's birthday! She wrote to me, and told me what a selfish boy he was, and how it was all my fault for taking him in in the first place."

"Is that what she said?"

"Yes, it bloody well is! And do you know why? Because according to John and Sissie – or my own precious flesh and blood, as she prefers to call them – I've been neglecting them in his favour since the day he arrived. Can you believe it?"

But Reg wasn't going to be drawn into a debate about who had said what behind Violet's closed doors. What Ma needed now was breathing space to work things out for herself. Would it help, did she think, if he invited Harold to stay on for the summer? He might even find him a little part in his opening production.

It was called *Women & Children First,* and it consisted of a collection of sketches based on popular scenes from Dickens, adapted by Reg to fit the available cast.

'*It is a far, far better thing that I do...*' That was Reg's own favourite scene, which would come at the end, of course, with Reg himself as Sydney Carton. But there would be plenty of opportunity to squeeze Harold in earlier.

Not as the Artful Dodger, though. That little morsel had been promised to Ian Maw, with twenty-year-old Trish as the ill-fated Nancy. And it wouldn't be David Copperfield, either, as Louise was threatening to play Dora even wetter than written, if Reg insisted on going ahead. But he did have a third alternative tucked up his sleeve – one he'd decided to abandon, when young Master Maw looked like getting a bit too big for his boots – and the scene in question was from *Great Expectations.* Louise would make a wonderful Estella, he was sure. And Harold...? The perfect Pip.

When Reg's proposition was put to Harold the following morning, he thought better than to jump at it, for fear of hurting Ma's feelings. But when she took him aside and insisted on the truth, he confessed to wanting it more than anything in the world. So it was settled, and all Ma needed now was to work out how she was going to explain his absence to John and Sissie in a way that satisfied three important conditions: one – that she didn't appear to know there'd been a conflict in the first place; two – that she should not be seen to be favouring any of her children over another; and three – that despite one and two, John and Sissie would end up believing they had come out the losers in an unequal contest. In the meantime, though, there was a victory to savour, and a happy fifteenth birthday in prospect for Harold next month, even if she wouldn't be sharing it with him. She was leaving him in good hands.

Louise, Trish…

It was nine o' clock on Monday morning, and Louise was off to buy herself an outfit for the funeral.

"Now are you sure you don't want me to come with you?" said Trish, but her heart obviously wasn't in it.

"No, I'll be fine," said Louise. "You'd only slow me down…and besides, I should think you could probably do with a bit of a break yourself, couldn't you?"

"What, from you? Don't be silly. But I still don't understand why you can't make do with that navy suit."

"Make do?" said Louise. "Now it's you being silly. First stop Tommy Tanner, I think…"

And with that, she kissed Trish on the cheek, and was off.

Poor Louise. She had never been comfortable in her off-screen skin – and a Tommy Tanner hat wasn't going to change a thing – but she never gave in to her insecurity, and it was with a feeling of deep longing that Trish stood at her living-room window, waiting for her sister to emerge into the street below. No Vincente Rossi to direct her down there.

Louise was out on the pavement now, pausing on the

kerb where two women were standing chatting – each with a little dog on a lead – and as she started to cross the road, she heard one of them say to the other:

"…She's only got to sniff one she's never come across before, and she has to go up and lick it."

"I know just how she feels, dear," said Louise, under her breath. But this was the real world, with no audience to overhear her, and from three floors up, even Trish missed her smile.

Heather…

Heather was alone in the Manor House for the first time since Tim's fateful excursion to the village shop on Friday night. Gerry had gone up to town – something to do with a new project he was working on, although he wouldn't say what – but he'd promised to be back by seven at the latest, and in the meantime there was Esther to be collected and settled in.

Heather had phoned her last night, and the arrangement was that she would pick her up at Salisbury Station this afternoon. Dave, the husband, would *not* be with her – Esther had been quite emphatic about that – so just the one bed to make up, and then plenty of time for a nice long soak in the bath before lunch. Funny, though, Gerry not wanting to talk about his project. He usually couldn't wait to let her know how clever he was. Still, if history was anything to go by, this latest idea would remain an idea, and next week there would be another one.

On her way upstairs, she paused in the hall, where she noticed the phone was missing from its base. Must have left it on the coffee table when she rung Esther last night. There was a small circular window alongside the front door, with a stained glass rose at its centre, which often mesmerised Heather when she was making a call. Her gaze was drawn towards it now, and there was a face pressed up against it, peering in at her.

Simon...

Simon was standing outside Canterbury Court, wondering whether to press the intercom button, or just let himself in as usual. He wasn't sure if Victor would be home yet.

On his way there he had bumped into Gerry Swallows, no great coincidence, as Gerry's London flat was round the corner from Victor's; but Simon had still come away feeling as if he'd been caught out. Gerry had invited him back, as he'd often done before, but this time Simon had made some pathetic excuse about Ronnie expecting him, and hurried away before Gerry could say anything that might change his mind. Now he couldn't even make the decision to let himself into Victor's flat. What was the matter with him?

Louise, Trish...

An empty box lay open at Louise's feet, the floor around it strewn with crumpled tissue paper; and on her knee... Tommy Tanner's latest masterpiece.

"Well?" she said to Trish. "What do you think?"

"I think it's absolutely gorgeous," said Trish, but she could see Louise was already beginning to have her doubts, if not about the hat itself, then about its appropriateness for the occasion. "Anyway, if you change your mind, you could always save it for Ascot."

"I won't be here for Ascot," said Louise. "Why? Do you think it's a bit…over the top…?"

"No…it's fine…"

"I mean, it is what Tim wanted, isn't it?"

"Apparently, yes. Oh, by the way, I hope you don't mind, but Esther phoned this morning, and I've invited her to stay for a few days."

"Of course I don't mind," said Louise. "How did she sound?"

"Bloody awful," said Trish. "And Dave won't be coming. I don't know what's going on there, but Esther's been staying with a friend for the last couple of nights."

"Poor thing" said Louise. "What time are you expecting her?"

"Oh, she's not coming today," said Trish. "She's staying with Heather tonight, and coming back with us after the funeral tomorrow."

"Well, in that case," said Louise, with a glance at her hat, "I think I'll go and try this on." And with that she disappeared into her bedroom.

But a few moments later she was back in the doorway, wearing nothing but a bra, a pair of pants and a conspiratorial look.

"I nearly forgot," she said confidentially. "You'll never guess who I saw today?"

"Who?" said Trish.

"Heather's brother. What's his name again?"

"Gerry," said Trish. "And you wouldn't need to ask

questions like that if you visited me a bit more often. He's become quite a celebrity over here lately."

"Has he?" said Louise. " I didn't even know he was in the business."

"He's not really. He's what you might call a media personality...you know, gossip columns, chat shows, that sort of thing...?"

"I know exactly the sort of thing," said Louise, trying to look disapproving. "He's a bit of all right, though, isn't he?"

"Do you think so...?"

"Oh...yes. Mind you, so was the young man he was busy chatting up..."

Simon, Alan, Victor…

The thrill of the chase – sexually speaking, that had always been the thing as far as Simon was concerned, and more often than not, the deed itself came as a bit of a disappointment. He and Ronnie hadn't shared a bed for years. Still, theirs was a long-term relationship, and the last thing Simon wanted was to get involved elsewhere, which was why as a rule the nearest he came to getting to know the men he played around with, was a few whispered words in some gloomy interior. Gerry Swallows was the exception.

To Simon's mind Gerry was the perfect physical specimen, and it didn't harm his case that Gerry fancied him too. They moved in the same social circles these days, and whenever they met – more often than not by chance – Gerry would invite Simon back to his flat, where they would start tearing at each other's clothes as soon as the front door was closed behind them. That was the one thing that Simon's relationship with Gerry had in common with all the rest – it lacked tenderness.

It was more than an hour now since Simon had met Gerry in the street, and turned down an invitation he would normally have jumped at – more than an hour since he had found himself standing outside Canterbury Court, wondering whether to press the intercom button or just let himself in.

An hour ago he had lost his nerve, and walked round to Gerry's flat after all, only to change his mind again, having rung the bell twice. He'd even heard Gerry's answer as he scuttled round the corner:

"Hello?"

Now Simon was in the lift on his way up to Victor's flat, having known all along that that was where he really wanted to be, but – more than that – hoping the delay had not brought Victor home. He was in luck. Alan had only just got in himself.

"I was just thinking about you," he said.

"Were you?" said Simon. "That's funny. I was thinking about you too. What time's Victor due home?"

"About nine, I think he said…but I'll be out of here by then."

"Why…where are you going?"

"I don't know…Carlisle, I suppose…if I haven't missed the last bus."

"But why?"

"Because there's no point in staying…is there? I mean, don't get me wrong, I've had a good laugh and everything, and yesterday was great…but then after you'd gone, I just thought…well, I came down here because I thought it would be different, but Vic's just like every other man I've ever met."

"I see…"

"I think I must give off this scent that attracts them."

"That attracts who?" said Victor, struggling into the room under an expensive-looking array of shopping bags. "Simon! Not again! Tell me, is it just my imagination, or have you moved in without telling me?"

But before Simon could answer, Victor had turned back to Alan, saying: "This scent that attracts who?"

"Oh, you know," said Alan. "Beggars…*Big Issue* sellers, that sort of thing. I took your advice today, and went out sightseeing."

"Did you?" said Victor. "Good. Well then, how about pouring your Auntie Poppins a nice big drink, while she goes and gets rid of this lot?"

And with that he disappeared into the bedroom with his shopping.

"Auntie Poppins?" said Alan.

"Don't ask," said Simon, before adding quietly: "And don't go…not yet."

"So…" Victor shouted to Simon from the bedroom. "What you wearing tomorrow?"

"What do you mean?" Simon shouted back.

"For the funeral."

"I'm not going to the funeral."

Victor reappeared in the doorway.

"Ronnie thinks you are."

"Oh, does he now?"

"Yes. I told him I'd pick you up at eleven."

"Right…well you get yourself there at eleven then, and I'll make sure he's ready."

Heather, Esther, Gerry…

Neither Heather nor Esther heard Gerry letting himself in. They were in the kitchen, where they had just finished preparing the vegetables for the evening meal. The joint was in the oven, and now they were sitting at the table drinking white wine, while Heather told Esther about this morning's uninvited guest.

"Hello…?" Gerry shouted. "Is anybody home?"

"We're in here!"

There was a puzzled silence out in the hall, and then Gerry appeared in the doorway.

"Esther!" he said, with a sympathetic smile. "No, don't get up…"

And before she could, he was leaning across the table to give her a kiss.

It could have been an awkward moment, but he got around it by saying:

"I hope that lot out there haven't been giving you a hard time?"

He was referring to the growing number of media people gathered at the front gate, but before Esther could answer, he noticed a bump on Heather's forehead, and said:

"Where'd you get that?"

"Oh, I just had a bit of an argument with the front door, that's all," said Heather.

"I wish it was all," said Esther, and then turning to Gerry: "Heather's been telling me about the man outside her bedroom window."

"What man?" said Gerry.

"You know?" said Heather. "The one in the waistcoat and bowler and stuff…?"

"Oh, yes…the paparazzo…"

"If that's what he was…anyway, the point is, he's back."

"I think you ought to tell the police," said Esther.

"Tell them what?" said Gerry. "That there's been a stranger hanging round the house for a couple of days? The place is crawling with them."

And then with another glance at the bump on Heather's head:

"What happened?"

"I saw him looking in at the hall window, so I went to ask him what he wanted, but unfortunately I opened the door too quickly, and cracked myself on the head."

"Did you knock yourself out?"

"No, of course not. I just swore. But it did take me a couple of seconds to get my act together again…and by that time he'd gone."

"And you're sure it was the same man?"

"Yes…!"

"Right…was he dressed the same?"

"I don't know. I only saw his face this time."

"We could check the CCTV, I suppose."

"I have."

"And…?"

"…And nothing…apart from a two-minute patch round about the time he was here, when the screen goes completely blank…and then it comes back on again after he's gone."

Simon…

Simon was in a good mood. He had had a couple of vodkas at Victor's, but that didn't matter, any more than it mattered that he had promised to be home by half past six at the latest, and now it was twenty past seven. He was seeing Alan tomorrow.

Victor had been intending to take Alan to the funeral, but in an inspired moment, Simon had mentioned that half the world's press would be there, and Alan had been quick to agree that he couldn't afford to risk an unscheduled appearance on the six o' clock news – not when he was supposed to be in the Lakes with his mates. So the plan now was that Alan would spend the day in Holland Park with Simon. Victor would drop him off when he picked Ronnie up in the morning, and collect him again when he brought Ronnie home. All perfectly innocent…

Louise, Trish…

"Trish?" said Louise.

"Mmm…?"

"Do you think Gerry *is* gay?"

"I've no idea," said Trish. "Why? Does it matter?"

"No, I suppose not. Still, it would be a waste…"

"Fancy your chances then, do you?"

"What, at my age? Are you kidding?" A short pause for

thought, and then: "On the other hand, though...it would make Max sit up and take notice, wouldn't it?"

"What would?"

"A photograph of me and Gerry out on the town."

Belinda, Jack...

Scene Three of *A Czech in the Post* was called *Solomon's Judgment*, and it opened with Jack sitting high on his throne, looking out across an empty stage.

A disembodied voice narrated:

"Then came there two women, that were harlots, unto the king..."

Enter Belinda from the opposite wing.

"...No, I said TWO women..."

At which point a curtain high screen slid noiselessly on to the stage, bringing with it a pre-recorded image of a life-size Belinda, walking towards her double. Same background, same fashion – same everything apart from the colour of her dress, which was red instead of blue – it always brought a round of applause, and another when the new arrival turned and spoke to the king.

"O my lord..."

"Hang on a minute," said the disembodied voice. "Now where was I? Oh, yes...two women, that were harlots, unto the king, and stood before him.

"And the one woman said..."

"O my lord," repeated the screen Belinda. "I and this woman dwell in one house; and I was delivered of a child with her in the house.

"And it came to pass the third day after that I was delivered, that this woman was delivered also: and we were together; there was no stranger with us in the house, save we two in the house.

"And this woman's child died in the night; because she overlaid it.

"And she arose at midnight, and took my son from beside me, while thine handmaid slept, and laid it in her bosom, and laid her dead child in my bosom.

"And when I rose in the morning to give my child suck, behold, it was dead: but when I had considered it in the morning, behold, it was not my son, which I did bear."

Belinda looked towards the audience and said:

"Nay; but the living is my son, and the dead is her son."

And the woman in red said:

"No; but the dead is thy son, and the living is my son."

"Ladies, ladies, ladies," said Jack, hitching himself up on his throne with one hand, and flourishing what appeared to be a baby in the other. "Just let me see if I've got this straight."

"Now you," he said, prodding the baby towards the woman in red. "You say this is your baby, and hers is the dead one?"

"Yes, my lord."

"And you," he said prodding the baby towards Belinda. "You say hers is the dead one, and this is yours?"

"Yes, my lord."

"Right," said Jack, with a self-satisfied look. "Bring me a sword."

"What are you going to do?" said both women together.

"I'm going to divide the living child in two," said Jack, "and give half to one of you, and half to the other."

"You can't do that," said Belinda.

"Yes, I can," said Jack. "I'm the king. I can do what I like." And then to the woman in red: "What do you think?"

"I think she needs help," said the woman, looking at Belinda.

"I think *he* needs help," said Belinda, turning to the audience.

"Yes, well all in good time," said Jack, continuing to address the woman in red, "but for the moment, what do you think to the idea of dividing the child in two?"

"Well, if you're serious about it, I'd rather you gave him to her."

"Aah," said Jack. "Now we're getting somewhere." And then turning to Belinda. "What about you?"

"I think she's right," said Belinda. "Give him to me."

"No, no, no," said Jack, using the baby as a gavel on the arm of his throne. "I mean, given the fact that I've got to decide which of you is the real mother, what do you say to the idea of half each?"

Belinda looked at him disbelievingly.

"You mean, you're hoping I'll settle for half a dead baby?" she said.

"Well, yes," said Jack. "How else am I going to demonstrate to the world how wise I am?"

"My God!" said Belinda. "You really do need help. Have you ever considered counselling?"

"Fancy a little nightcap later?" Jack asked Belinda, when the curtain came down on the first act.

"Better not," she said. "Early start in the morning, and I've got a funny feeling Rod might be waiting up for me tonight."

"Fair enough," said Jack. "Will you have time to drop me off though, do you think?"

Simon, Ronnie, Queenie…

Queenie Delaney would never get used to the idea of her son sharing his life with another man, but on the other hand, it didn't cost anything to be civil – or at least not as much as it would cost to come out the loser in a showdown for her son's affections – so she did try. And once a fortnight she came for dinner.

"How's the new job going, Simon?" she said.

"It isn't actually…yet," said Simon. "We start rehearsals on Wednesday."

"Oh, yes, I think Ronnie did tell me. What's it called again?"

"*Naval Reserve.*"

"Which reminds me," said Ronnie, jabbing his fork at Simon. "Have you made up your mind yet what you're wearing tomorrow?"

"Why?" said Queenie, clutching gratefully at the change of subject. "What's happening tomorrow?"

"Tim Court's funeral," said Ronnie, and then to Simon: "Victor's picking us up at eleven, by the way. Did I tell you?"

"No, but he did," said Simon. "And the latest plan is that he's picking *you* up at eleven, and I'm staying here to keep an eye on his friend."

"Which friend?" said Ronnie.

"You know…the one from Friday night," said Simon. "He can't go, for some reason or other…"

"I'm surprised you're going yourself," said Queenie to

Ronnie. "After the disgraceful way Timothy treated our family. He'd have been nothing without us…"

Esther…

Esther couldn't rid herself of the idea that the man Heather had described earlier – standing in the lane outside her bedroom window – had sounded exactly like Harold's character, Gabriel in *Shotgunning*. But she'd kept quiet about it, because she didn't want to trigger another exchange about the events of Friday night, and *Shotgunning* had been on television when Tim's death was announced.

She'd have preferred not to have to discuss her beloved son at all – at least not with Heather and Gerry, whose sincerity she had doubted since the first time she met them. Like the Manor House itself, they always made her feel uneasy, but as she didn't believe in ghosts, she was probably wrong about the house; so maybe she was wrong about Heather and Gerry too.

As for the man in the lane…well, he couldn't have been Harold, or Heather would have recognised him, surely…? And with no actual evidence to demonstrate his existence, Esther had been forced to agree that it would be a waste of time to contact the police.

Belinda, Jack…

In the car, on the way home from the theatre with Belinda, it was Jack who broke the silence.

"You're very quiet tonight, Linnie," he said. "There's nothing wrong, is there?"

"No," said Belinda. "I was just thinking…"

"What about?"

"Tim…"

When Belinda Lucas met Timothy Court on a Hollywood film set, he was already a star, and she was a comparative newcomer, but they were both English, and soon struck up a friendship, which Belinda should have recognised as being different from her usual working relationships…but didn't.

Tim was tall, dark and married, which ticked all Belinda's boxes, so at the very first opportunity, she manoeuvred him into a corner where she could make herself available to him…

There was a table in the corner – a candlelit table for two, which Belinda had reserved specially – and it was here, over a light meal and a bottle of the Napa Valley's finest, that Tim turned her down.

It was something that had never happened before, and with nearly half a quart of Schramsberg bubbling away inside her, Belinda persuaded herself that Tim was just being polite – so she tried again. But what had seemed like a generous offer first time round, now started to sound like a sales pitch – not only to Tim, but to Belinda herself – and she knew the game was up.

So she apologised, and Tim accepted, but when he dropped her off at her apartment later that night, she apologised again, and the next morning she awoke to a feeling of apprehension that kept her lingering in bed far later than usual.

From that night on, Belinda burned with outrage and shame every time she thought of Timothy Court, and the fact that he carried her secret around with him – the only man who could be sure of her dubious morality, without sharing the burden of it. Belinda usually suffered pangs of guilt after a night with one of her lovers, but they would always fade once she had managed to convince herself that Rodney wasn't going to find out; and without fail the dread she felt on the late night drive home would dissipate by morning. No one was going to give her away – not without giving himself away too. But with Tim it was different.

To make matters worse, Tim seemed determined to continue with the friendship, in fact to cultivate it further. Back in England, Belinda was introduced to his wife and friends, and even Rodney was drawn into the circle, all of which made her feel more and more uneasy. Worse still, she had to pretend to be enjoying it.

Tim never once mentioned her indiscretion to her, but often when she found him looking at her, it seemed to her that it was with a degree of understanding and forgiveness that amounted to condescension. She did not want to be understood! She did not want to be forgiven! She just wanted it not to have happened. If only it hadn't happened. If only he was dead. And now he was.

"Were you very friendly with him?" said Jack.

"We were quite close, yes."

"Meaning what?" said Jack.

"Meaning don't ask a question, unless you're sure you want to hear the answer…Tim taught me that, actually."

Cassie, Larry…

There was a thirty-year old myth at Calumet – still popular today – about a star-struck teenager, who had woken up one morning, to discover that the man who looked down on her from the poster above her bed, had come to life and moved in next door.

It was 1968, and Harold Masters was driving from Southampton to Norfolk, when a couple of hitchhikers caught his eye, and he stopped to give them a lift. They were on their way back to Kent from the Isle of Wight, and they flattered Harold into making a detour, by telling him how jealous their daughter was going to be, when she found out who had picked them up. She even had one of his posters on her wall, her father said…and her name was Cassie.

A few days later, Harold did move in next door, but there were no posters on Cassie's wall – just a photo under her pillow – and no room in her heart for anyone but Larry Duncan Campbell.

To this day Larry and his wife, Jacqueline lived in the house at Taylor's Farm, which was the nerve centre of the Foundation, and the place where Larry had introduced Cassie to the joys of sex on her sixteenth birthday.

She was forty-six now, and they were celebrating the thirtieth anniversary of that momentous occasion, in a hotel in Canterbury, where Larry was sound asleep in bed, and Cassie was lying next to him…wondering how Harold was getting on.

Tuesday, 21

The Vicarage,

18th September, 1946

Dear Harold,

It is only a week or so since you left, but it seems a lot longer, because we are all missing you so much. Everybody is still talking about your great acting debut, particularly Reg, who says you rose magnificently to every challenge he threw your way. Tilly says he is incapable of using one word when ten will do, but of course she would never change him. None of us would.
   The surprising news is that Blatch Robinson has left the company…

It was as close as Esther had ever come to criticising Reg – or anyone else for that matter – as she tended to rely on this second-hand way of expressing her opinions: Tilly says this…none of us would that…

But when it came to facts, she was much more direct, and it would be from Esther that Harold learned about Trish's departure for the States in 1947, and Louise's decision to join her there three years later.

In the meantime, though, he visited his Norfolk family as often as he could, and although the school holidays were their busiest time, and there was always work to be done both on and off stage, he couldn't get enough of it.

It wasn't usually possible for Reg to fix him up with a part of his own, but Harold never complained. Instead he learnt every line of every production the Players ever put on, so that he was ready to stand in when the occasion arose, more often than not for Ian Maw, but for the other men too, and even for Reg himself once, when his health let him down with the company at full stretch.

It was Reg's health that would eventually lead to the Players' disbandment in 1951, when his wartime experiences finally caught up with him, and he had a mental breakdown; but until then he kept the show on the road with an enthusiasm that had everyone dancing to his tune…

"Dancing to his tune…is that what we were doing?"

This is what Harold is thinking, as he turns left out of the gates of Calumet in his Daimler DS420, having read Esther's letter again less than an hour ago.

It's the summer of 1946 – Ma has gone back to London – and Oliver is showing Harold round the Allingham Estate, when he says:

"I'm not a bit like the others, you know? In fact Reg often says he paid the midwife to swap me. It's his way of telling Trish and Louise they're getting on his nerves;

and when I'm getting on his nerves, he says he wishes he hadn't bothered."

Harold doesn't know what he's supposed to say, so he says:

"Does he know you call him Reg?"

"It was his idea. Tilly objected at first, but he always gets his way in the end…you'll soon learn that."

Tilly has given them a picnic, and they're sitting on the riverbank eating it, when Oliver says:

"I think I'm a bit of a disappointment to him, actually."

"Why?" says Harold.

"Oh, lots of reasons…my lack of interest in the theatre, for one thing. I caught him looking at me the other night, as if he really did think I'd been swapped at birth, but I'm afraid that's one thing he can't do anything about. He'll enjoy having you around, though…"

Harold is sharing Oliver's bedroom, and that night when they're getting undressed, Reg comes upstairs to say goodnight. After he's gone, Oliver says:

"I hate the thought of letting him down, you know. He's had such a hard time of it."

And then, with a shrug of the shoulders, he jumps into bed, and says:

"Still, I'm sure everything will come out right in the end. I'll introduce you to Esther tomorrow."

Esther turns out to be Oliver's girlfriend, and for the rest of the summer the two of them and Harold spend most of their spare time together – by the river and on the river, or sometimes in one of the caravans Oliver is helping to renovate – talking, reading, playing cards…

Towards the end of Harold's stay, Tilly remarks how

125

lucky it is that they all get on so well, and Reg says he could not agree more. Then on Sunday he surprises everyone by announcing he's coming to church with them.

Esther's father is the Vicar of May, and his text this morning is taken from Galatians, Chapter Six:

> 'Be not deceived; God is not mocked: for whatsoever a man soweth, that shall he also reap.'

Harold notices that whilst Oliver appears to be totally absorbed by what the Reverend Bradbury is saying, Reg is becoming more and more agitated with every word, and Tilly has to nudge him in the ribs to make him sit still. Not his sort of theatre, obviously – so why did he come?

After the service, Reg invites Esther to the cottage for lunch, during which he embarrasses her by calling her 'my favourite future daughter-in-law'. Tilly tells him off for that, but Harold can see from her expression how much the idea appeals to her. And perhaps to Esther too? Is that what her blushes mean? It's a question that still haunts him nearly fifty-two years later, but the reality is that he never asked it, and Esther did marry Oliver.

My favourite future daughter-in-law…was that one of the challenges Reg threw his way?

Louise, Trish…

Louise was standing by the window, looking out for the car, which wasn't due for another twenty minutes.

"Come and sit down," said Trish. "You're making me feel nervous."

Louise glanced at the clock, and decided against a cigarette.

"I wonder how Esther's getting on with Heather?" she said.

"I wonder," said Trish. "It can't be easy for her, can it…particularly if you're right about how she feels about her?"

"What…about her being a gold digger, you mean?"

"Mmm…"

"You don't think she'll say anything, do you?"

"Are you kidding? She wouldn't say anything if she suspected her of murder. Why do you think she married Oliver?"

"I don't know. Why?"

"Because she was too polite to drop him, when she fell in love with Harold…that's why."

"Funny," said Louise. "I always thought she married him out of loyalty to Reg."

Victor, Alan, Simon, Ronnie…

Trish and Louise had been on the road more than half an hour, by the time Victor and Alan rolled up at The Rondel – the house in Holland Park Ronnie and Simon had shared for the last ten years – and Ronnie should have been ready. But when the doorbell rang, he was still in his bedroom, struggling to pin a trio of tiny daffodils to his lapel – so it was Simon who saw Victor first.

He was wearing a sage green suit with a lavender pinstripe, and mustard coloured shirt, tie, socks…and even shoes.

"Well?" he said, with a triumphant grin. "How do I look?"

"I love the Jimmies," chuckled Simon. "Are you sure you know what you're doing?"

"Just following instructions," said Victor. "And if you think I'm pushing it, make sure you're watching the news this afternoon."

"Why?"

"Never mind why. Just think Nijinsky…or Nureyev, at his provocative best."

"Sounds intriguing. Are you coming in?"

"No, thanks. We're running a bit late." And then nudging Alan forward: "I'll swap you this one for an old one."

"Hang on. I'll just get him."

"I'm here," said Ronnie, appearing alongside Simon, wearing a smile he'd been preparing for Alan all morning. And then he spotted Victor's shoes.

Louise, Trish…

In the car on the way to Denby Green, Louise said:

"I wonder if Harold will be there?"

"I doubt it," said Trish. "I don't think he's set foot out of that Calumet place in thirty years."

"No…strange business, that. Do you really think Esther was in love with him?"

"I think she probably still is."

"Do you? What about Dave?"

"Well, she certainly isn't in love with him. Anyway…"

A slight movement of the driver's head had alerted Trish to the fact that it might be a good idea to change the subject.

"...I know who will be there," she said. "Victor Andrews...remember him?"

"Unfortunately, yes."

They'd met him at a party to celebrate Heather's first television appearance – although bizarrely, Heather herself had pulled out at the last minute. But Tim had been there – and Esther – and it was the last time Louise had clapped eyes on either of them. It was the *only* time she'd ever clapped eyes on Victor, although she'd heard a lot about him, and been curious to meet the man who'd managed to tempt Tim away from the Delaneys. That was why she'd allowed herself to be cornered by him when he made his approach...but she hadn't got her answer.

"A good contract's worth more than any number of good scripts."

That was the only revealing thing he'd said during their short conversation, and she'd despised him for it – then steered clear of him for the rest of the evening. Strangely enough, she'd noticed that Tim himself had had very little to do with the man either. She'd intended to ask Trish about it at the time, but never got around to it.

"What are you thinking?" said Trish.

"Eh...? Oh, nothing much," she said. "I was just wondering how Tim managed to get mixed up with a man like Victor in the first place."

The funeral...

By eleven o' clock quite a crowd had gathered outside the Church of All Saints', Denby Green, although the media outnumbered the public by about two to one.

One day soon there would be a memorial service – in fact Heather was already toying with the idea of the Abbey – and no doubt that would attract thousands of Tim's loyal followers from far and wide; but for the moment, apart from the press and a limited number of invited guests, virtually everyone from further afield than Denby Vale was unaware of the occasion – despite its colourful nature.

Like Ronnie, most of the male mourners had decided to play it safe, with a buttonhole of spring flowers, or a brightly patterned tie, the outstanding exceptions being Victor in his pin stripe, and Gerry in an off-white linen suit, expertly cut to fit in all the right places.

Among the women, it was Louise who stood out, in a stunning combination of lemon and plum, with Heather at her most demure in a pale pink mohair sheath.

And finally, there was a faun – or a youth dressed up to look like one – a protégé of Victor's, whose semi-naked beauty would continue to disturb more people than cared to admit it, long after the clatter of hoof on stone had ceased to echo around the walls of All Saints'. It was a publicity stunt, of course, although the culprit would never admit it, and within hours his image would be syndicated to every news organisation in the developed world.

Afterwards the congregation left the church and assembled at the graveside, forming an arc there, which curved out from the minister's left hand, in an ever-widening sweep down one side of the grave. Was no one willing to face the others across the void? Or were they all expecting someone to come along and take a group photograph?

Heather, Esther and Gerry took the most prominent

positions, nearest the minister. Victor and Ronnie came next — Victor having deliberately left a wide enough gap between him and the leading trio to be able to comment on the proceedings without being overheard, while Alan's substitute, Jamie — an old standby, hastily telephoned last night, and picked up on the way down this morning — hovered a yard or two further back, and tried to brazen out the shame he always felt when he was out in public with Victor. He often wondered if Victor was aware of that shame. It seemed unlikely that he could be, without toning himself down, and yet sometimes Jamie got the impression that Victor could read his every thought. As if to underline this, Victor turned and winked at him now, just as he was manoeuvring himself into a position where he would have a clear view of Gerry Swallows. Because Alan wasn't the only one to have succumbed to a certain video ploy, and just as five tireless gymnasts started making their way across Jamie's mind's eye, towards a room where two men in evening dress were removing another's kit, there was Victor winking at him, as if he knew exactly what was going on.

Belinda and Rodney came next in line, Belinda keeping half an eye on Rodney to see if he was looking to see where she was looking, Rodney keeping half an eye on Gerry Swallows to see if he was looking at Belinda. Trish and Louise stood furthest of all away from the minister, so that they had the most comprehensive view of the proceedings — albeit in semi-profile — two old-stagers, watching from the wings for once.

As for the rest of the mourners...well, they were gathered in uneasy bunches behind the front line, waiting for the proceedings to begin.

Most of them were nervously rearranging some part of their clothing, or coughing politely in anticipation of the ceremony. But not Gerry…or Heather…

"Doesn't she look lovely?" Trish whispered to Louise.

"They both do," said Louise, and Trish wondered if her sister was thinking what she was thinking.

"They could almost be the bride and groom, couldn't they?" she said.

But Louise didn't have time to answer. The committal was about to begin.

"Man that is born of woman," droned the minister, "hath but a short time to live, and…" with a quick look at the congregation, "…and is full of misery. He cometh up and is cut down like a flower…"

"…A daffodil," said Victor under his breath, but if Ronnie heard him, he pretended not to.

"He fleeth as it were a shadow, and never continueth in one stay…"

Rodney thought he saw Belinda shiver, and moved in closer, to put a comforting arm around her. Perhaps it was turning chilly, despite the spring sunshine.

"Thou knowest, Lord, the secrets of our hearts…"

Victor glanced at Ronnie, whose expression betrayed not the slightest hint of conscience, even having confirmed in the car on the way to pick Jamie up, that he had indeed had an affair with Tim a few years ago, although he hoped he could count on Victor's discretion, as he'd only told Simon in the heat of an argument, and never intended it to go any further. Ronnie could feel Victor watching him, and he summoned a tear to the relevant eye.

"For as much as it hath pleased Almighty God of his

great mercy to take unto Himself the soul of our brother here departed, we commit his body to the ground."

Heather was staring at the freshly dug grave, quite oblivious of Gerry's admiring glance. The most important thing now was to see her performance through without distraction, and the way to do that was to focus on something. The hole in the ground seemed as good as anything.

Esther thought only of Tim. Nothing could have distracted her – least of all the idea that at this very moment her husband might be lighting up a cigarette, his hands cupped against the breeze, before stepping inside the Regent to join his cronies for a drink.

"Earth to Earth, ashes to ashes, dust to dust…"

A shrill laugh rang out across the churchyard, and everyone turned towards Louise, because they were in no doubt that she was the culprit. Years before, many of them had heard that same shriek used to brilliant effect in her Oscar-nominated portrayal of the Bitch of the Buchenwald. Here, a moment earlier, she had experienced an odd sensation of unreality, and for an instant she had imagined herself an outsider, a stranger looking down on this colourful arena, rather than an actress playing her own part in it.

In an effort to explain the feeling, she had turned to Trish and whispered:

"You know, this whole thing's so…so…unlikely…I wouldn't be a bit surprised if Tim himself suddenly appeared, and told us it was all some sort of elaborate joke."

Everyone had been far too busy following the progress of three token handfuls of dirt, to notice Trish nodding towards the grave, as she leaned over and whispered in her sister's ear:

"Well, darling, if he's going to, he'd better get a move on."

"I hear a voice from Heaven saying unto me, Write…"

It was nearly over. Just a few prayers, and then it would be back to the house for a drink. Heather looked up at last. Had she done the right thing by ignoring Louise's outburst? She was inclined to think so; certainly Esther hadn't reacted. Heather was aware of Esther at her side now…aware of her, but no more, because if anything, Esther was a pace or two behind her, just out of her line of vision. Gerry too…and yet she was perfectly conscious of his every movement.

Then there were the others…well the main players anyway. Apart from the minister, Heather couldn't actually see any of them; but she knew not just who they were, but where they were, and how they were standing. Was it a heightened sense of perception brought about by…by what? The occasion? A prolonged period of intense concentration? Or had she made an unconscious mental note of where everybody was, even before the committal began?

She was staring straight ahead of her now, at an oak tree, which stood in a corner of the churchyard beyond the grave. Funny there was no one over on that side. But even as she thought it, a man stepped out from behind the tree…

The minister was approaching his close with misgivings. He had the most awful feeling that this strange group of people was going to hail his performance with a hearty round of applause.

Imagine his relief then, when the widow groaned, half-buckled, hovered on the brink of consciousness, her arm outstretched towards the grave, and then collapsed at his feet. Normality restored, he rushed off the last few words of the proceedings, just to keep things tidy, and then lent a sympathetic hand in getting the poor, pale woman to her feet.

Simon, Alan…

Simon was propped up in bed, his left hand caressing the back of Alan's neck, while with his right he was pointing the remote at the television in the corner – channel-hopping in the hope of finding a bit of funeral footage.

When he finally got there, he was just in time to see a half-naked youth emerge through All Saints' lych gate, only to be swamped by a tidal wave of photographers.

"Who was that?" said Alan, sitting up and taking notice.

"I don't know," said Simon, his eyes still fixed on the screen. "But I bet I know a man who does."

"Who?"

"Victor, of course…I just wish he'd been as savvy when I was that age."

"What do you mean?"

"I mean, it's a set-up. You heard what he said about Nureyev, didn't you? Well now we know what he was talking about. You wait…by this time tomorrow, that little fucker will be getting more headlines than the guy they've just buried."

"Well, good for him," said Alan, snuggling back under the duvet. "I know who I'd rather be."

The wake...

"That was a master stroke if ever I saw one," said Gerry about an hour later.

Esther had insisted on putting Heather to bed, while Gerry helped Victor with the rest of the guests, but at the first opportunity he had abandoned the party and come upstairs to his sister's bedroom. She was sitting at her dressing table, brushing her hair.

A master stroke?

"What was?" she said, as if she really didn't know.

But there was no fooling Gerry.

"The fainting fit, of course," he said. "I'm not kidding, Sis, you've got them eating out of your hands down there."

Heather looked puzzled for a moment, and then turned towards him in disbelief.

"You didn't see him, did you?" she said.

"Who?"

"The man in the churchyard...over by the tree."

"Sorry, I'm not with you."

"It was him, Gerry...the one who's been prowling round the house all week."

"What...the one in the waistcoat, you mean?"

"Yes."

"And where was he again?"

"Right bang in front of you...about twenty feet away. I just don't understand how you managed not to see him. Esther said she didn't either, but I wasn't sure whether to believe her or not. Have you seen her at all?"

"Yes of course...just before I came up. She was with Trish and Louise."

"And how did she look?"

"Exactly how you'd expect her to look…sad…a bit bewildered…"

"But not suspicious?"

"No, of course not. Why would she look suspicious?"

"You didn't see the way that guy was looking at me."

"No…and neither did she apparently."

"No…"

"So…how *was* he looking at you?"

"As if he knew what I was thinking…how I felt about Tim…everything…"

Downstairs Esther was on the point of telling Trish and Louise what had caused Heather to faint, when she spotted the vicar alone in a corner, and excused herself, intending to go over and thank him. But on her way, she overheard Rodney telling Belinda about a car he'd seen parked near the church. The car of his dreams, apparently – a Daimler DS420 – and Belinda stifled a yawn, and took another sip of sparkling water, and everybody was behaving as if the incident in the churchyard had never happened.

Upstairs Heather was trying to persuade Gerry that someone was bound to have seen her uninvited guest, and if they had, wouldn't they have been shocked by his appearance, and that stare of his, which had been so knowing, it had actually caused her to faint?

Not at all, insisted Gerry, who knew better than to suggest she'd imagined the whole thing. After all, Victor's shoes were yellow, so why not a gold waistcoat…? And how much more offbeat could you get than a vision from heaven with the hind legs of a goat? His logic was irresistible, and by the time he'd finished talking, Heather was ready to rejoin the party.

Downstairs Victor had the vicar where he wanted him – in a corner, within arm's reach of a plateful of delicious-looking cakes.

"To call homosexuality a sin," he was saying, "is rather like calling breathing a sin, don't you agree? Silly, because like breathing, it just can't be helped.

"Whereas to call a sexual act a sin, would be more like saying it was a sin to eat, wouldn't it? Equally silly, but it could be argued, I suppose…"

And then, reaching for the plate of cakes:

"Do you fancy a dainty?"

Jamie was on unfamiliar ground. He had long since tired of trailing around at Victor's heel, having failed to keep him entertained beyond a quick mince behind some dotty old bird in the hall, when he thought no one was looking; and if he was normally what you might call cocksure, at the moment he was far from it, having drawn a blank with Gerry too. He sought consolation at the buffet, and was helping himself to a generous measure of champagne from a bottle he had found abandoned there, when he realised he was being watched.

Louise felt a bit mean about it, having caught him in the act of pouring himself a drink he obviously didn't believe he had any right to, when she'd only been thinking how lonely he looked; so she smiled him a reassuring smile, and even raised her glass to him, inviting him to come and fill it, and make her a partner in crime.

But Trish had been watching Jamie too, having spotted him from the landing earlier, mimicking Louise's walk for

Victor's amusement. In its own grotesque way, that little charade had reminded Trish of what she had moved back to England to escape – a game in which too many ageing Hollywood divas were being escorted around the party circuit by men half their age, while being parodied from coast to coast by every female impersonator capable of putting on a wig half straight. Most of the escorts were as gay as the drag queens, and although Trish had nothing against men who fancied men, she had no more intention of becoming the butt of their ridicule, than she did of becoming an amusing conversation piece at one of their dinner parties.

It was a subject she'd often thought it might be wise to discuss with Louise; but with Max still around it hadn't seemed necessary to give the matter top priority, and rather than risk starting an argument now, she made some excuse about going to rescue Esther, and left Louise to it.

Five minutes later – having failed to find Esther – she glanced across the room, fully expecting to see her place filled by Jamie, with Louise playing up to his every sycophantic word; but she was surprised to see him back where she had first spotted him – at the buffet, helping himself to the dregs from another conveniently abandoned bottle – and Louise where she'd left her, a picture of defeat. She went over and sat down.

"What happened to your friend?" she said.

"I'll tell you what happened to him," said Louise with feeling. "I sent him off with a flea in his ear, that's what!"

"Why? What did he say?"

"Well, for a start, he asked me who I was, which didn't help."

"Oh, dear," said Trish. "You mean, he didn't know…?"

"Know!" said Louise. "He didn't even know when I told him!"

Belinda was sitting by herself in a corner. Rodney had gone off to find the bathroom, and it did cross her mind to get up for a wander, but she decided against it in the end. He'd be back in a minute, putting two and two together, so it was probably wiser to stay where she was. At least Gerry had kept out of the way. She'd spotted him a few minutes ago, talking to a faun in an alcove by the fireplace, but now he was at an even safer distance – helping Heather choose some music.

"Hello, Belinda. You're very quiet."

It was Victor, she was delighted to see, because even Rodney couldn't suspect her of fancying a go at him.

"Hello, stranger," she said, moving up to make room for him. "I like your shoes."

"Thank you," he said. "And where's that handsome husband of yours?"

"Having a pee, as far as I know," and then, surveying the room: "I see Ronnie's still up to his old tricks…"

Victor followed Belinda's gaze, to the buffet, where Ronnie was mounting an assault on Jamie.

"I don't know," he said. "You turn your back for five seconds…"

"Oh, I shouldn't think you've got much to worry about there."

"Why do you think I'm sitting here…? Hey, you'll never guess what the old sod told me this morning, though."

"Go on…"

"Only that he'd had an affair with Tim Court, that's all."

"What…? You are joking…aren't you?"

"I wish I was," said Victor. "But as God is my witness, he'd barely had time to park his wrinkled old bum on my nice new upholstery, and out it all came in the most intimate of detail."

"Oh, please," said Belinda. "I've just eaten…"

But then another unpleasant thought occurred to her…

"Victor…?" she said. "I don't know quite how to put this, but…what would you say if I told you I'd had an affair with Tim?"

"Oh, no, not you as well. How many more…?"

"No, seriously, darling, please…just for instance. What would you say? Would you start going on about my wrinkled old bum, or is it just the idea of it being Ronnie that makes it so hard for you to swallow?"

"I'm not sure I know what you mean," said Victor.

"I mean, are we talking about Tim's taste, or his…virtue?"

"Are you trying to tell me there really was something going on between you?"

"Let's just say there easily could have been."

"What happened? Did he turn you down?"

A stinging slap, and once again Victor was the centre of attention.

"What now?" said Heather to Gerry, as Belinda stormed out of the room; and Trish remarked that it was getting more like a wedding every minute.

But Louise didn't hear her. She was trying to recall something – an item on the news the day after Tim died, when a few of his friends had been rounded up to say nice things about him. Only Belinda had managed to hint at something more than nice…and now here she was drawing attention to herself again…and Gerry was following her out into the hall.

He found her in the kitchen, where she was still shaking with anger – not at Victor any more, but at herself for having hit him – and she couldn't apologise enough. What must poor Heather be thinking? But Gerry put his arm around her shoulder, and told her it had been Heather who had sent him to find her. She wanted her to come back and finish Victor off.

Esther had reappeared meanwhile, and was explaining to Trish and Louise that she'd been in her bedroom, trying to contact Harold on her mobile phone…but without any luck. The trouble was that Harold didn't own a phone of his own, and in the past she had always reached him through his neighbour, Cassie. But Cassie wasn't answering, and the only other number she had was for the so-called father of the community – a man called Larry Duncan-Campbell – who lived in the main house. But according to his wife, he was away; and the wife had been confined to the house for days apparently, so she had no idea whether Harold was on site or not.

Having got all that out of the way, Esther said:

"Do you remember that lovely old car he had?"

"*I* do," said Louise. "He gave us a lift back to town in it, after…"

"After what?" said Trish.

"After Tim's christening," said Esther. "No, Lou, please don't apologise. I want to be reminded. It was a Daimler, wasn't it?"

"Was it? No…no, I'm pretty sure it was a Jag."

Upstairs Rodney was faced with a real dilemma. A bathroom door without a lock was guaranteed to render his bladder watertight at the best of times; but in this houseful of shirt-lifters…

After five fruitless minutes he had no choice but to seek outside help – from his late mother – and back it came, as it invariably did, the song she had always sung to coax open her son's biological valves…

"Wee Willie Winkie…" it went, and 'Wee Willie Winkie' was what he sang now, very quietly of course, with one eye on his potential aim, and the other on the door handle, straining the while for the tell-tale fairy tread of a predatory pansy on the landing outside.

And it worked, eventually, his dear old mother's song; but even so, it was a hot and flustered Rodney who arrived back in the living room five minutes later.

Belinda wasn't there, but Victor and Heather were standing in the corner where he'd left her, and he was on his way over to ask them if they'd seen her, when the sound of a familiar voice behind him made him turn in his tracks. Belinda and Gerry were framed in the doorway, Gerry with his arm around Belinda's shoulder, and Belinda giggling guiltily at something he was whispering in her ear.

They didn't see him coming – not until a split second before the punch landed – and by the time Gerry managed to pick himself up off the floor, Rodney was dragging Belinda down the garden path, and making it clear to the waiting photographers exactly what would happen to them if they didn't get out of his fucking way.

Simon, Alan...

It had been quite a day of discovery for Simon. For instance, he now knew that Alan was due to take his A-levels in a couple of months, and had been provisionally accepted at three universities, one of which was Sussex. In fact he'd been invited to an open day there in a few weeks' time, and he had a feeling Sussex University wasn't too far away from London. Just outside Brighton, he seemed to remember it was. Was Brighton quite near London?

That was one of the things Simon admired most about Alan – his openness. When it came to admitting what he didn't know or understand, he just came out with it, never mind what anyone might think of him. And he was right. What did it matter? Although Simon doubted that Alan ever thought it through in that way. On the other hand, he wasn't completely artless. After all, if it hadn't been for one or two hints on his part, they wouldn't be where they were now – in Simon's bed, having missed lunch. Simon couldn't have cared less about lunch. No one had ever fallen asleep in his arms before.

Alan had made a few discoveries about Simon too – that he was instinctively suspicious of a compliment, for instance – and on a more trivial level, that despite his sexual orientation, he wasn't very keen on musicals at all...apart from the likes of *Cabaret*, that is, where the routines were performed as staged set pieces, and the cast weren't required to sing their way through breakfast. The other thing he liked about it was the fact that despite the quality of the singing and dancing, the director still succeeded in making you believe it was all taking place in some seedy back street dive, and not where it deserved to be – on Shaftesbury Avenue.

"Bloody Hell!" said Alan, when he heard all this. "And I thought I liked it, because it was good."

That was another thing Simon admired about Alan – his quick mind. He was more savvy than he let on, and quite capable of holding his own in any company…so why had he spent the best part of his first visit to London moping around Victor's flat? It didn't make sense. Unless perhaps – like Simon himself – Alan just needed the right person to bring him out. Better wake him up before Ronnie came home.

Rodney, Belinda…

Rodney didn't realise it, but he'd done Belinda a favour by dragging her away from the Manor House, because now he would never hear about the slap she'd given Victor, and she wouldn't have to come up with a reason for having done it. On the other hand, she wasn't going to thank him for it, and they were ten minutes out of Denby Green before she could bring herself to speak to him.

"Well," she said finally. "Are you going to tell me what that was all about?"

Silence.

"Look," she said more gently, lifting his left hand off the steering wheel, and placing it on her belly. "I can't afford to get myself in a state at the moment, so…I'm just going to tell you this once more and for the last time. There is not, and there never has been, anything going on between me and Gerry Swallows. We do bump into each other from time to time, yes, and when we do, we usually have a laugh, but there's nothing underhand about it – it's just the business we're in – and I am not going to hide myself away from every vaguely attractive man under sixty in order to bolster your fragile ego. Do you understand?"

"Yes."

"Good…because I mean it, Rod. And tomorrow morning you can bloody well phone him and apologise, and…"

Belinda was on a roll, and tomorrow morning she would be on the telephone herself – to Rosie Fallon, the woman who was collaborating with her on her autobiography – asking if it was possible to make a few changes. Might as well milk the situation for what it was worth, and with Tim underground, the way was free at last for her story to be told the way she wanted it to be told.

But she'd developed the idea further since her chat with Victor, and if Rod didn't like it, he was just going to have to lump it.

An innocent abroad – that was how she was going to describe herself now…

> *I'd never worked in the States before, and I was finding it a bit hard to adjust…until Tim Court took me under his wing.*
>
> *Two or three days after I arrived he invited me out for dinner, and of course I accepted. Just another friendly gesture from a fellow Brit, was the way I looked at it, and as the pair of us had spent every minute of our spare time going on at great length about how much we adored our partners, there seemed to be no harm in it.*

We had an early start the following day, so we went easy on the wine — just half a bottle between us — and then rewarded ourselves with a brandy each over coffee. And that is the last thing I remember, until I woke up in his bed the following morning.

Tim was up by that time, and feeling much better than I was, bringing me coffee in bed, running me a bath, offering me breakfast, and dropping me back at my own place in plenty of time to get changed before my car arrived. No one saw us, and I'm certain he never mentioned what had happened to anyone, because there were no amused glances, no sly digs…and when I turned down his offer of another date he accepted my decision with good grace. The perfect gentleman, then — or so I thought — and we remained good friends until the day he died.

In fact it was hearing about his death that prompted me to tell a close friend about what had happened between us. I just wanted to talk about him, and I knew I could rely on my friend's discretion, so I told her the whole story, including the fact that I had no recollection of anything that had happened from the moment we left the restaurant until the moment I woke up in Tim's bed several hours later.

And didn't I find that odd, she said, bearing in mind how little I'd had to drink…?

Well, yes but…

Had I never heard of Rohypnol…?

No, I hadn't…

The rape drug.

End of story. Rosie would help her with the grammar.

Louise, Trish…

Esther was in bed. Louise had offered to move in with Trish, so that she could have a room of her own, and she had accepted gratefully; but although it was nearly midnight now, and the day had been a long one, neither of the sisters was showing any inclination to follow her example and turn in, because each of them still had something to say.

"So," said Louise. "What's the verdict on Gerry, then?"

"Regarding what?" said Trish.

"Regarding whether he's gay or not."

"Well, Belinda's husband clearly doesn't think so."

"No…"

"And I wasn't at all surprised when he hit him, you know. Did you see the way he was looking at him in the churchyard earlier?"

"Not really, no. I was too busy looking at him myself, to be honest…and Heather, of course."

"Mmm…they did paint a pretty picture, didn't they?"

A long pause, and then:

"Louise?"

"Yes?"

"Gerry and Heather…they are definitely brother and sister, aren't they?"

Cassie, Larry…

Cassie had more reason to distrust Larry than his wife did, because – unlike Jacqueline, who had nothing to go on but her own insecurity – Cassie knew exactly what he was capable of...more than thirty years of infidelity.

It was the second day of their stay in Canterbury, and Larry's legitimate reason for being there was a three-day series of talks he was giving on psychic phenomena.

Jacqueline couldn't be with him, because she was confined to the farmhouse at the moment, with an undiagnosed condition, which she described as ME, and Larry described to Cassie as hereditary hysteria.

That was the true Larry, Cassie's demons tried to persuade her, and not the one spouting mumbo-jumbo in the Empress Suite downstairs. But the two weren't necessarily incompatible. Everyone had a dark side, after all, and it must mean something if Larry allowed her the occasional glimpse of his.

Tonight's talk was about astral projection, a practice which Larry described in his book as *'one of the most liberating experiences open to mankind'*. It involved a separation of the spirit from the body, and a journey into a dimension known as the astral plane, where one could wander the universe at will, observing, listening...

A liberating experience for some, no doubt, but to Cassie it sounded more like a handy way of poking your nose into other people's business...if it really was possible.

By now Larry would have finished his prepared lecture, and would be inviting questions from the floor. But like the majority of people who attended his workshops at Calumet, most of his audience would be fully paid up converts, and he was a master at turning the tables on hecklers. He should have been a politician...or a comedian.

Astral projection...was it really mumbo-jumbo? Cassie

was inclined to think so, but then unlike her parents, she had been a sceptic since she was capable of independent thought. And yet she loved living at Calumet, for all its New Age pretensions. And she was sure she wasn't alone in that. It wasn't just enlightenment they came there in search of. It was refuge…from the real world.

"Like the Foreign Legion, this place," Harold had said once. "But with Shamanic rattles instead of guns."

When Larry came up to the room, he was shaking his head with disbelief. But at what? Had he been found out?

"How did it go?" said Cassie cautiously.

"Brilliantly," he said. "In fact it couldn't have gone better if I'd scripted it myself."

"I thought you did," she said.

"No, not the talk," he said. "The question and answer session afterwards."

"Why? What happened?"

"Well," he said, flinging himself backwards on to the bed. "There was this guy in the audience…I recognised him actually. He lives in Ashurst, I think…somewhere round there, anyway…and he wanted to know if it was possible to travel in time as well as space. I told him he'd know the answer to that if he'd read my book, but then he said he'd only discovered me a few days ago…when he found my method on the internet, and thought he'd give it a try."

"Right…"

"So…he had a couple of unsuccessful goes, and then bingo! At the third attempt he was flying. But no sooner had he left his body than he came across this other bloke, dressed like a character in a film he'd seen when he was a kid. One or two of the audience had a chuckle at that, but I'm not kidding, Cass, you could see even they were lapping it up."

"And what about you?"

"What? Did I believe him, you mean? Yes…absolutely!"

Cassie studied him carefully for a few seconds, and then said:

"So…what happened next?"

"Well," said Larry. "This is where it gets even more interesting, because he couldn't remember what the film was called – or the year it was supposed to be set in – but he reckoned it was a Western, so we're probably talking late nineteenth century. Then some joker in the audience shouted out: 'What was he then, this guy you saw…a cowboy or an Indian?' And that did get a laugh. But our man didn't miss a beat. He just turned on him, and said: 'Look, pal, for all I know he was a fucking accountant on his way to some astral fancy dress party, but I saw him…all right?' And then he walked out."

Wednesday, 22

Dearly beloved, avenge not yourselves, but *rather* give place unto wrath: for it is written, Vengeance *is* mine; I will repay, saith the Lord.
Romans 12:19

1950, and having completed his National Service, Harold enrolled at the Central School of Speech Training and Drama, much to the amusement of his brother, John, who thought all actors were nancy boys, and had no idea Ma was stumping up the fees. She was paying for Harold's accommodation too – a second floor bedsit in a house in Oakley Street – and he'd found himself a part time job in a pub nearby. The Central School of Speech Training and Drama. Harold had Reg to thank for that – in fact he had a lot to be grateful to the Court family for – and in December Oliver and Esther came down to visit him.

The news they brought with them was that Louise had been signed up by one of the big Hollywood studios, and would not be coming home. Another nail in the coffin of the Norfolk Players – that was how Oliver described it – and it gave him no pleasure; but he couldn't see them surviving beyond next season, and even Reg's enthusiasm was beginning to wane. But enough about that. It was Friday night, and they were here to enjoy themselves…

On Saturday Harold had to work at lunchtime, but he'd managed to get the evening off, and he arranged to meet the others outside Lyon's Corner House at six in the evening. In the event, though, he was ten minutes early, so he wandered into Leicester Square, where he came across Esther, sitting alone on a bench.

"Hello," he said. "Where's Oliver?"

"Oh, I told him I wanted to do a bit of shopping," she said. "So he left me to it."

"Good," said Harold. "Do you mind if I join you?"

"Don't be silly."

Harold sat down, and put his arm round her shoulder, which took her by surprise, but she didn't object, and after an awkward second or two, she said:

"Well…look at us."

"I know," he said, leaning over and kissing her on the cheek. "The orphan and the vicar's daughter…who'd have thought it, eh?"

And who knows where their conversation might have led, if they hadn't spotted Oliver walking towards them, clutching a handkerchief to his face.

He hadn't seen them, and there was nothing in his manner to suggest anything amiss, but distress has an uncanny way of transmitting itself, and both Harold and Esther were on their feet before they noticed his bloody nose.

"Oh," he said, when he recognised them. "I was hoping…I thought we were supposed to be meeting outside the Corner House, weren't we?"

"Yes, well never mind that now," said Esther. "What happened?"

"Someone punched me…"

"What?" said Harold. "Who…when?"

"Just now," said Oliver. "These two lads jumped me, and took my wallet…"

"Where?"

"In an alley down there…"

"Did you see which way they went?"

"No…"

"Oh, come on, Ollie, you must have done…"

"Harold, please…" said Esther. "Leave it…"

And before he could protest any further, a man carrying a sandwich board appeared out of nowhere, tripped over on the pavement right in front of them, and fell down at their feet.

A few days later – when Oliver and Esther had gone back to Norfolk – Harold received their Christmas card, with a note from Esther tucked inside it. And this is what it said:

Dearly Beloved,

I want nothing more than for all of us to be happy, so please avenge not yourself, but rather give place unto wrath – and forgive him: for it is written – right here – that I am glad Oliver stopped you going after those men; and it is not cowardly to back away from a fight you can't win.

Did you like your present? I hope you got it, or this letter will not be making any sense at all. Oliver chose it of course, but I chose the bookmark, so whatever you think of him, you must think of me too.

Romans, Chapter 12, on a sandwich board in Leicester Square – you couldn't make it up, could you? But he really does believe it, you know? And I think I do too. It helps me to sleep in an unjust world.

Having said that, my hero, your gallantry helps too. So thank you, from a damsel no longer in distress,

Esther

Nearly half a century has gone by since that letter was written, and there is a Holy Bible in the trunk under Harold Masters' bed, with a bookmark inside it, which has been there so long it's stuck to the page. Somewhere on that page there is a verse, which begins:

'Dearly Beloved…'

Heather, Gerry…

Heather was in the kitchen cooking breakfast, when Gerry came down.

"I'd forgotten about those photographs in your bedroom," he said.

"Which photographs?" she said.

"You know…the portraits you had done when you got back from your honeymoon…? Oh, you need bog paper, by the way. I had to nick some of yours."

"Right…one egg or two?"

"Two, please. I love the one of you."

"What? Oh, the photograph…? Yes, it's all right, I suppose."

"Poor Tim didn't stand a chance really, did he? I'll tell you what, though. I can't help feeling a bit uncomfortable under his gaze now that he's dead."

"Sorry…?"

"The photo of Tim…I said I can't help…look, there's nothing wrong, is there?"

"Eh? Oh, no…I was just thinking about that business in the churchyard, that's all…" and Heather shifted the frying pan off the heat for a moment. "I still can't believe nobody else saw him."

"Yes, well as I said, maybe they did, and they just didn't bother to mention it. I mean, by the way you described him, he didn't exactly look out of place, did he?"

"No, I suppose not."

"So…are you going to cook those eggs or what?"

Heather put the frying pan back on the hob, and said:

"Do you still think he's paparazzi?"

"Yes I do…what else?"

"I'm not sure. You don't think he's stalking me, do you?"

"Are you serious?"

"Why not? It does happen, doesn't it?"

"Well, yes, but from what little I know about them, I wouldn't have thought a stalker would show up while the place was crawling with photographers and security men. He'd wait until the commotion died down."

"Mmm…I suppose."

"Look, let's just give it another day or so, eh…? Let the dust settle a bit…"

Gerry walked over to the window and nodded in the direction of the drive, at the end of which the world's press had been gathered since Saturday morning. There were only three or four die-hards left now.

"They'll be gone by this evening," he said. "So…if he shows up after that, we'll do something about it…promise."

"All right," said Heather, dubiously. "But I still don't fancy spending the day here on my own. I don't suppose you feel like keeping me company, do you?"

"Sorry, Sis, I can't today. I've got to go up to town again later."

Trish, Louise, Esther…

There was something unnatural about the atmosphere around Trish's breakfast table this morning, and it had everything to with the question Trish had put to Louise late last night.

"Gerry and Heather…" she had said. "They are definitely brother and sister, aren't they?" And about two seconds later Esther had popped her head round the door.

"Do you think she heard?" Louise had whispered, after they'd all said their goodnights for the second time; and Trish had had to admit that she honestly didn't know.

Now Louise was too chirpy by half, as if by prattling on, she could distract them all from the implications of Trish's question. Trish, on the other hand, was quieter than usual, taking occasional sips of coffee, while her toast grew cold in the rack, and her third cigarette of the morning lay smouldering in the ashtray.

Esther thought of Dave, and how often the smoke from

his cigarettes had been enough to put her right off a meal. And yet Trish's smoke wasn't bothering her at all. It was the man she despised, not the habit. Time to clear the air.

"Louise," she said politely. "I'm sorry to interrupt, but would one of you please tell me what on earth is the matter? It's not Dave, is it?"

"What makes you say that?" said Trish.

"Well something's obviously wrong," said Esther. "And as the pair of you have spent the last two days avoiding the subject, I just wondered if that was it. Oddly enough, I spent the whole day yesterday wondering when I was going to have to explain away his absence, and yet nobody else mentioned him either."

"Too embarrassed, I should think," said Trish. "And speaking for myself, I got the impression that that was what you wanted."

"Oh, I'm not complaining," said Esther. "Just making an observation, that's all. And I noticed no one said anything about the Swallows clan either."

"The Swallows clan?" said Louise.

"Heather's family," said Trish, and if this was as close as she was going to get to knowing whether or not Esther had overheard her last night, it was also an ideal opportunity to find out more.

"They weren't at the wedding either, were they?" she said.

"Oh, so you did notice then?" said Esther, with mock indignation. "You know, you're such a self-centred lot, you theatre people, I sometimes wonder if you ever notice anything that isn't your own reflection in a mirror."

Trish smiled warmly.

"Do you know?" she said. "Those are the most welcome words I've heard from you in a long time. But never mind about that now. Tell us about the Swallows…"

"Well…" said Esther, and although she didn't realise it, she had reached an important landmark in the grieving process. This wasn't the first time in the last few days that her burden had grown temporarily lighter, but it was the first time she hadn't felt guilty about it.

Her story began in London in the early 1950s, with two brothers – Arthur and Ben – whose father wanted them to join the family business.

"Tarpaulins, he was in, I think," said Esther, but Trish was inclined to believe she knew a lot more about it than she was letting on.

"Anyway, Arthur was the first one to disappoint him, when he went off and joined the merchant navy at seventeen; and then a few months later, his younger brother, Ben, got his girlfriend pregnant. Mary, she was called.

"Of course, in those days pregnancy usually meant marriage, and I suspect Ben planned the whole thing, because he knew Mary's parents were pretty well off, and whatever they thought of *him*, they weren't going to let *her* go short, were they? Not with a baby on the way. So that was what happened. Ben and Mary got married, Mary's father set them up in a little flat, and Ben settled down to a life of complete idleness.

"The really odd thing is that Mary didn't seem to mind. In fact she indulged him to such an extent, that even the children began to suffer. Oh yes, I nearly forgot to tell you…Heather was the result of that first pregnancy, and she was barely weaned before Gerry was on the way."

At this point in the story, Louise couldn't help but cast a guilty glance in Trish's direction, but Trish pretended not to notice, and Esther carried on.

"I wouldn't go as far as to say they were neglected, but they weren't loved…not by their parents anyway."

"Arthur used to visit them when he was on leave, though, and before long, he left the sea, came home, and set himself up in a little sweet shop not far from where they lived. Clapham, I believe it was…or rather is…they're still there actually."

"What?" said Trish.

"Well, not Arthur," said Esther. "He's dead…and you know about Heather and Gerry…but Ben and Mary are still there."

Trish wanted to ask questions, but Esther hadn't finished yet.

"Anyway," she said. "The kids soon started spending more time with Arthur than they did with their parents, and eventually they moved in with him."

"Just like that?" said Louise. "Didn't anyone object?"

"Well, Ben and Mary certainly didn't."

"How extraordinary."

"I know."

"And Ben and Mary are still there?"

"Yes."

"Doing what?"

"Nothing…actually they couldn't now, if they wanted to, because Ben's been bedridden for the last few years, and Mary never leaves him, except to go shopping and so on…certainly not to go to her daughter's wedding…or…or Tim's funeral…"

"And what does Heather think about all this?"

"I don't know. She's never mentioned them…"

"So…how did you find out about them?"

"Tim, of course," said Esther…and then blushing: "Well, to be honest, I did make a few enquiries of my own when he told me he was getting married."

"You did what?" said Trish. "I can't believe it."

"I know," said Esther, sheepishly. "I quite surprised myself actually. But it all happened so quickly."

"Mmm…" said Trish. "And what else did you find out?"

"Nothing…of any significance."

A second or two for everything to sink in, and then Trish said:

"How did Arthur die?"

"In a car crash," said Esther. "He'd been down to the south coast somewhere to see a clairvoyant…a woman he'd been going to for years, apparently. He was quite a one for that sort of thing – you know, crystal balls, tarot cards, astrological charts, and so on. He never set foot in the church over the road, but he was perfectly happy to drive halfway across the country to have his palm read."

"And then he crashed his car after visiting a clairvoyant. There's a joke about that, isn't there?"

"Oh, yes, " chuckled Esther. "I see what you mean. But actually I always wondered if it was what she told him that *made* him crash. Anyway, the important thing is that I didn't uncover anything damning about Heather…"

"…And the wedding went ahead."

"Yes."

"Do you like her?"

"Not much, no. But I couldn't tell Tim that, could I? He was besotted with her."

"What about Gerry?" said Louise. "How do you feel about him?"

"The same way I feel about her, funnily enough…only more so. I mean, he's always perfectly charming…"

"But…?"

"But I wouldn't trust him as far as I could throw him. And the thing is, he likes it that way. It's a game he plays. Did you see the look of mischief on his face yesterday, when Belinda's husband hit him? I don't know whether he'd done anything to deserve it or not, but he obviously wanted the husband to believe he had…even if it did mean a punch on the nose."

"Oh," said Louise. "I wish I hadn't asked you about him now."

"Why?" said Esther.

"Because he's taking me out for dinner tonight."

Simon, Alan…

The rehearsal studios were situated in a side street off Long Acre, but having given Alan the address, Simon had funked it at the last minute, and arranged to meet him outside Covent Garden underground station as close to one o' clock as he could. That was if he could get away at all.

Alan had said he would wait all day if necessary, and at half past one he was beginning to wonder if that was going to be the case. Talk about frustrating. Less than thirty-six hours from now he was due back in Carlisle, and already they'd wasted one precious night to avoid arousing suspicion. Now it looked as if they were going to miss out again – and then what?

They had started making plans yesterday afternoon, but Simon had barely got as far as explaining where Covent Garden was, before Victor had arrived back from the funeral with Ronnie, and whisked Alan away.

Now Simon was standing on the steps outside the rehearsal studios, chatting to his director, as if he had all the time in the world, which he would have after tomorrow, if he didn't get his act together soon…all the time in the world to grow old with a man he didn't love.

It was nearly two o' clock when he made his escape, and ran all the way to the tube station, where he found Alan trying to conjure him up by turning round slowly on the spot three times.

Ten minutes later, they were sitting in the Crusting Pipe, sharing a sandwich and a bottle of wine.

"So," said Simon. "How did you get on last night?"

"Oh, you're all right," said Alan. "Nothing happened."

"No, I didn't mean that."

"Yes, you did."

"All right, I did. So how did you manage to keep his grubby little paws off you?"

"Easy. I just persuaded him to join me in a spliff, that's all."

"A spliff?" said Simon. "Are you kidding?"

"No…why?"

"Because for one thing, he hasn't allowed *me* to strike so much as a match in that flat, since he gave up smoking."

"No, well he wouldn't let me either, until I told him what the side effects were likely to be."

"And what were they likely to be?"

"That it would knock him spark out. That's not what I told him, of course, and I made the first one really weak, so that he'd think it wasn't having any effect. It's the only way to do it, according to this guy I know in Carlisle. Let them think they can handle it, so they end up wanting more. Then you roll another one, only this time you make it much, much stronger, and before they know where they are, they're completely out of it."

"And is that what happened?"

"Yep. I went for a pee, and by the time I got back he was sound asleep on the settee. So I put a duvet over him, and he slept right through."

"What about this morning?"

"Don't know. By the time I got up, he'd gone."

"Good."

"Mmm…I don't know how I'm going to hold him off for another night, though."

"You might not have to. Ronnie's staying with his mother tonight, so if we can come up with a convincing story for Vic…"

Alan thought about this for a moment, and then said:

"It's a pity we can't just tell him the truth."

"I know," said Simon. "And we will eventually, but if we tell him now he'll go straight to Ronnie…and if you and I really are going to get it together…"

"We are, aren't we?"

"I hope so…but if we are, I'd rather break the news to Ronnie myself."

Another pause for thought, and then Alan said:

"I know…what if I tell Vic I've got to go home a day

early? I could say I phoned my mum to see how she was, and she's been taken ill, and wants me to go back straight away."

Simon looked a bit more hopeful.

"That could work, I suppose."

"Then I could pack my bag, stay with you, and go straight from your place to the coach station tomorrow, before Ronnie comes home. What do you think?"

"Let's just concentrate on today, shall we?" said Simon. And then, looking at his watch: "Talking about which I'd better get back."

Louise…

In a recent interview in an American slimming magazine, Louise had been asked how she felt about the ageing process, and her answer had been that she believed in growing old gracefully. And it was true. It was also true that she was often described as looking young for her age, or beautiful…for her age, but that was not the same as looking young and beautiful, and she knew it.

She tried to make the best of herself – the best of what she already had, that is – so botox and collagen injections were out of the question, as was cosmetic surgery of any description, and at seventy years of age, she applied her make-up in the same way as she had done at twenty – thinly.

Her skin was lightly tanned, her hair auburn-tinted. Had it gone grey she'd have left it grey – or so she tried to persuade herself – but in fact it had changed colour gradually, unevenly and unpleasantly, and become streaked with a sort of dirty yellow, which reminded her of nicotine stains, so the tint was a necessity and nothing to do with vanity.

Her teeth were capped and white and even – it had been the norm in the Hollywood of her day. Now she noticed that a lot of the younger women in the business kept their own teeth as part of their individual look…and a good thing too. To Louise's mind that represented one little step forward for the woman in a man's world…the very fact that some of them were allowed to keep their teeth. Still, if there was one thing about her own teeth for which Louise would remain eternally grateful, it was the fact that they were at least to be found where they should be – in her mouth – and never in a glass by the side of her bed. Her sight was good, her heart was good, and if her outline was always well covered these days, it still looked good in silhouette.

There was one other respect in which the years had failed to change Louise – and that was that she could not look in her wardrobe without discovering she didn't have a single thing to wear.

Belinda…

Belinda was on the phone to Rosie Fallon, the woman who was ghost writing her autobiography.

"I want to change something," she said.

"Right…"

"Don't worry…it's nothing major. I just want to add something to the chapter about Tim Court."

"Sounds interesting."

"It is. Can we meet?"

"Yes, of course. How about tomorrow morning?"

"Perfect…oh, no, I can't. I've got an appointment…" With her GP, Doctor Holman…

"Nothing to worry about," he'd said, when she drew his attention to a rash on her lower abdomen, the day he confirmed her pregnancy. "But we'll do your bloods sooner rather than later, shall we…just to be on the safe side?"

And she'd hardly given it another thought, until half an hour ago, when his secretary had phoned to ask her to come in first thing tomorrow.

"And I've got a matinee in the afternoon," she said to Rosie now. "What about Friday?"

Louise, Trish…

If looks could kill, the latest assistant in Louise's once favourite dress shop would have been lying on her face in a pool of blood, having brought Louise a cat suit to try on.

"I like it," said Trish.

"You buy it then," said Louise. "It would take me a month to get into it."

"Nonsense," said Trish. "There's room for two of you in that. Mind you, I'm not sure what you'd do if you were caught short."

"Right, that's it!" said Louise. "Come on…coffee."

And it was over a cappuccino and a cigarette or two that Louise finally got around to telling Trish about her dinner date.

"I was going to tell you last night," she said. "But I didn't want to say anything in front of Esther. And then, just as

I was getting around to it, you dropped your bombshell about Heather and Gerry."

"And Esther did hear me, didn't she?"

"Do you think so?"

"Oh, come on, Lou. Why do you think she chose this morning to tell us their life story? All that business about Heather hardly being weaned before Gerry came along…as if she'd just thought of it, when she'd probably been lying awake half the night trying to think of a way of putting me straight without embarrassing me. Anyway, never mind that now. Tell me about tonight."

"There's not a lot to tell, really…apart from the fact that I wish I wasn't going. Did you see the look on Esther's face…?"

"Oh, I shouldn't worry too much about what Esther thinks. She's hardly in a position to point the finger, is she?"

"Isn't she? Oh, you mean Dave?"

"Exactly. On the other hand, I'm still not convinced that being seen with a man like Gerry is the right way of putting the spark back into your marriage."

"Nor am I."

"So, why did you ask him out, then?"

"I didn't. He asked me."

Alan, Simon, Victor…

Alan had decided to take the easy way out, and leave before Victor got home, but the mild feeling of unease he felt while he was getting ready, turned to complete panic, when he discovered he'd lost the piece of paper Simon had written his address and telephone number on. All he could remember was that the house was called The Rondel, and it was in a district called Holland Park…no road name, and not a clue as to how to get there.

Having searched in vain for an address book, and found nothing familiar in the phone book under Daly or Delaney, he was just beginning to wonder if he was going to have to confront Victor after all, when he noticed the telephone on the hall table. It was one of those phones that could be programmed for automatic dialling, and inset into the back of it was an index card, on which were written the names of the dozen or so people Victor contacted most frequently. Simon's name was at the top of the list.

Alan picked up the phone and pressed AUTO 1.

Simon answered – "Simon Daly…" – and Alan breathed a sigh of relief.

"It's me," he said.

"Alan…? Is everything all right?"

"It is now…or at least it will be when you've reminded me where you live."

Minutes later, and in between chuckles, Alan was in the middle of writing down Simon's address, when he heard Victor's key turning in the front door.

"Got to go," he said, before he could ask for Simon's phone number; and Simon recognised the situation by the urgency in his voice.

"Right," he said. "Get a taxi when you're ready. I'll pay…"

And they hung up.

"Who was that?" said Victor, coming into the room.

"My mum," said Alan, and in the couple of seconds it

took him to add that he had something to tell Victor, and he'd be back in a mo, Victor had clocked the piece of paper he was folding and putting in his pocket, his haversack on the floor in the corner with his jacket draped over it, and the fact that he was avoiding eye contact in exactly the same way as he had when they got back last night. What was he up to?

Victor had his suspicions, and while Alan was out of the room, he picked up the telephone and pressed REDIAL, only to have them confirmed.

"Simon Daly…"

"Simon!"

"Victor! You sound surprised."

"I am. I thought I was phoning someone else. Must have pressed the wrong button. Everything all right?"

"Yes, fine."

"Good. Sorry, I can't talk. I promised to phone this client the minute I got in, and he'll be waiting to go out himself. I'll speak to you later, okay?"

"Okay…"

"Bye then…"

And Victor put the phone down, just as Alan walked back into the room.

"So," he said, "what did Mum have to say?"

"She's not well," said Alan. "So I said I'd go home tonight…"

"Aah, that's a shame," said Victor, his plan already formed. He knew exactly what was going on now, and not just because of the piece of paper, the haversack, the lack of eye contact and the telephone call, but also because Ronnie had mentioned on the way home from the funeral yesterday that he was spending the night at Queenie's tonight, and staying over, in order to be on hand to take her to hospital first thing in the morning. Victor had a feeling it wasn't Queenie he was planning on staying with at all, and the only reason he'd gone to the trouble of mentioning it was as a sort of reinforcement of his alibi should Simon decide to check up on him…but that was another matter. The important thing now was that Ronnie was going to be away from home for the night, leaving Victor with a betrayal of his own to have to deal with.

"I thought she thought you were in the Lakes," he said.

"She does," said Alan.

"So how did she get my number?"

"She didn't. I phoned her."

"Oh, I see. Just as well, by the sound of it. Pity, though. I had a nice little surprise lined up for you tonight."

"Did you?"

"Yes. Ronnie and Simon were going to give us dinner at their place."

"*Were* they?"

"You sound surprised…did you have a premonition about your mother, by the way?"

"What do you mean?" said Alan, and Victor pointed at the haversack.

"I just wondered how you knew to pack your bag, that's all."

Alan looked puzzled.

"It was already packed when you spoke to her on the phone."

"Oh, I see what you mean…no…I…er…I had to ring

Victoria, to find out what time the coach was, and she asked me to ring her back."

"Right…" said Victor. "And what time is it?"

"Half seven…talking about which, I'd better get a shift on. Do you mind if I phone for a taxi?"

"Don't worry. I'll drop you there on my way to Ronnie's. I suppose I might as well still go."

"Don't you need to get changed?"

"What…for Ronnie and Simon? I don't think so. Come on."

Louise, Trish, Esther…

Louise was in her room getting ready, while Trish did her best to put Esther in the picture about her date with Gerry.

It had transpired in the coffee shop earlier that Gerry really had been the one to suggest dinner tonight, and Louise had accepted, not because she was hoping the news would get back to her husband, but because he'd asked her within earshot of the 'little squirt' who'd had the cheek not to recognise her at the funeral. She had spotted the said squirt making eyes at Gerry earlier, and seen accepting as a way of getting even with him. That, Trish had said, explained everything perfectly. But as Esther pointed out now, what it didn't explain was Gerry's reason for asking her out in the first place.

Victor, Alan, Simon…

A holiday romance. That would have been the politest way of describing what had gone on between Victor and Alan for the past week, and the atmosphere in the car on the way to the coach station was oddly in keeping with that myth, in that not a lot was said, but the few things that were, supported the illusion that their relationship had a future.

"I'll try and take a bit of time off next time," said Victor at one point, and Alan would have felt guilty if he hadn't been fairly sure that Victor had rumbled him…all those questions in the flat about who he'd been phoning and so on. The trouble was he didn't dare admit anything in case he was wrong.

Victor's, on the other hand, was an even more delicate predicament, because if he wanted to stop Alan and Simon making a complete fool of him, it was essential they remained ignorant of the fact that they'd been found out, or they might still end up spending Alan's last night together, having convinced themselves they had nothing else to lose.

It was for this reason that Victor decided not to accompany Alan into the coach station. There was no coach, of course, or if there was, Alan had no intention of catching it, but to confront him with either of those presumptions would be to risk forcing him into the open, and that would not serve Victor's purpose at all. So he decided to say his goodbyes in the car, and tried to imagine what he would do in Alan's shoes.

Alan, in the meantime, was wondering what he was going to do if Victor did decide to come into the coach station with him. It was too much to hope that there really was a nineteen-thirty to Carlisle, and even if there was…

Victor decided that in Alan's place he would phone

Simon at the first opportunity, in which case there was only one option open to him – to get in first. That was why he overshot the station by a good few yards, and having said his fond farewells, was on his mobile before Alan could reach the entrance.

"Simon Daly…"

"Simon…it's me…"

"Vic…!"

"There's no one with you, is there?"

"No. Ronnie's out. Why…what's up?"

"Alan's run off with my wallet."

"What?"

"Yes. He spun me some yarn about having to go home a day early – because his mother was sick – and when I got back from dropping him off at the coach station, it had gone."

"You dropped…Victor, are you sure?"

"Of course I'm sure. Do you think I haven't searched the place a thousand times? Twelve hundred quid, I had in that wallet, not to mention all my credit cards and stuff. I thought he seemed a bit funny when I offered to drop him off, but I didn't think any more about it till we got there, and I saw him talking to this bloke."

"What bloke?" said Simon.

"I've no idea," said Victor. "But he looked as if he knew him, if you know what I mean…and then I saw him handing him something. What do you think I should do, Si…phone the police?"

Trish, Esther...

With Louise out of the way, Trish suggested a game of cards, and it was while she and Esther were reminiscing over a hand of knockout whist, that – for no reason she could think of – she felt compelled to ask about Dave, and Esther's decision to marry him.

"Just call it a moment of madness," said Esther. "What the defence would describe as the balance of my mind being disturbed."

"The defence?" chuckled Trish. "You haven't bumped him off, have you?"

"No, but I wish somebody would. Come on...your deal."

Trish took the hint, and they played on in silence, until a moment or two later, Esther trumped Trish's ace with a five, and Trish said:

"There was a time when you'd have given me that."

"Never..."

"Yes, there was. I can remember you playing a seven to my queen once, and I knew you had the king. I was...what are you laughing at?"

"Trish, it must be fifty years since you and I played cards..."

Esther was in the middle of dealing the next hand, when Trish said:

"Anyway, I like it."

"What?" said Esther.

"The new you. It used to annoy me the way you always let Oliver have his way."

"I did not."

"Yes, you did." And then, realising she was in danger of going too far: "I bet you wouldn't have trumped his ace."

At two tricks apiece, Esther said:

"I did love him, you know?"

"I know," said Trish.

"And Tim couldn't have asked for a better father."

"No…"

"But you don't get your name in lights for being a good father…do you?"

"See what I mean? You never would have said that fifty years ago." And then slapping her last card down on the table: "Now, then…pick the bones out of that."

Alan…

What to do next? That was Alan's dilemma. Victor had presumed he would phone Simon the minute he reached the sanctuary of Victoria Coach Station, and – given the chance – that's exactly what he would have done. But his last call to The Rondel had been on automatic dial, and Victor had interrupted that before he could ask Simon for the number.

He had managed to scribble down the address before he hung up, but Victor was probably there himself by now, so no question of rolling up at that front door. And if Ronnie really had invited them for dinner, that must mean he'd changed his overnight plans too, so the coast wouldn't be clear until tomorrow at the earliest…possibly not then.

On the other hand, Simon was due at the rehearsal

studio in the morning. Perhaps he could wait for him there.

Louise, Gerry…

Yet another busy night at Alfredo's Trattoria, and the first opportunity two particular waiters had had to talk to each other since last Friday.

"I wouldn't mind *him* trying to eat me in a darkroom," said the first one, nodding towards the man sitting at table eleven.

"Well, I'm blowed," said the other, "…if you'll pardon the expression."

"Do you know him then?"

"Of course. That's the infamous Gerry Swallows. And have you seen who that is with him?"

But the first waiter could only see the back of the woman's head.

"It's not Julie Andrews, is it?" he said.

"No. It's Louise Court."

On the way to the restaurant, Louise's driver had put her in mind of a man she'd made a film with when she first went to Hollywood, and before long she'd found herself daydreaming about how good Gerry would look in a Republican Army uniform. But she'd also had an entire day to ponder on Esther's opinion of him, and by the time she'd reached her destination the brave young soldier, immaculately turned out and ready for action, had metamorphosed into a scavenger, picking his way between the bodies on some long-abandoned battlefield, and pausing only to tread the blood-streaked face of a corpse into the mud, before ripping the crucifix from its neck with a smile. Now, about two hours and three or four glasses of Orvieto later, the Swallows charm was beginning to work its magic, and Esther and her opinions were all but forgotten. But there was still one question that Louise needed an answer to.

"Why did you ask me out?" she said.

"Does there have to be a reason?" said Gerry, lighting a cigarette. He'd asked for permission before he smoked his first one, and Louise, who should have been flattered if anything, had wondered instead whether he'd have done the same thing had she been twenty. Now she just accepted it. Did there have to be a reason?

"Actually," said Gerry a few minutes later. "There is a little favour I'd like you to do for me, if you would."

"Oh yes?" said Louise.

"Yes…well, not so much for me as for an old friend of mine. Have you ever heard of a man called Meredith Parker?"

"Of course," said Louise. "I've worked with him actually."

"You haven't?" said Gerry.

"No, on second thoughts, forget I ever said that. He must be in a home by now, isn't he?"

"Not exactly, no," grinned Gerry. "He's appearing in cabaret in this dinner joint in Islington."

"What…singing, you mean?"

"Well…that's what it says on the poster, yes…and as I'm supposed to be promoting him, I wondered if you and Trish might like to be my guests there on Saturday night? Effinelli's, it's called."

So that was it, and it was with a stab of disappointment that Louise realised Gerry was simply hoping to use her name to boost Meredith's attendances. On the other hand, though, if that was all he wanted her for, why the dinner tonight?

The truth was that Gerry had sunk quite a lot of money into Effinelli's latest venture, but Meredith Parker wasn't an old friend of his at all, and the decision to bankroll his comeback had been a strictly commercial one. True to form though, Gerry had been far too sure of himself to bother with any homework, and that was why the disaster that was Meredith's performance had surprised him too late to back out of the agreement.

The show was in its second week now – although to everyone involved it seemed like years – and apparently the public were staying away in droves; but Gerry was nothing if not an optimist, and over the weekend an idea had occurred to him about how to turn what seemed like an irredeemable stroke of bad luck into a platform from which to launch his own future career. He would take Meredith's place.

Gerry had always fancied himself as a modern-day Sinatra, but until now, he had only scratched the surface of his showbiz potential, with no more than a handful of television chat shows to his credit. No singing as yet, and despite his frequent appearances in the celebrity mags and gossip columns, no producer had come forward with an offer to exploit his talent further. Now, though, he was suddenly in a position to do it himself – on a very small scale, it had to be admitted – but even that need not necessarily be a disadvantage, if the seats were all occupied by the right people.

His biggest challenge so far had been in getting Merry to agree, which he'd tried to do by describing it as an exercise in damage limitation. But Merry's was a much bigger ego than that. All the more surprising then, that what had done it in the end was the list of potential punters Gerry had lined up for Saturday night – a list that was headed by Patricia and Louise Court. One sniff of that, and Merry's resolve had crumbled immediately, leaving Gerry with nothing further to do than perfect the short but inspired set that was going to project him into another dimension.

"Yes, we'd love to come," Louise was saying now. "But that's not the only reason you asked me out, is it?"

And she was right of course. Gerry could just as easily have made the arrangements for Saturday night at the funeral or over the phone, but in Louise's case he had been looking way beyond Islington, and to his mind the idea of a powerful friend in Hollywood had more than justified the price of a meal at Alfredo's.

Now Louise seemed to be hinting at something more than that. But was it really possible the old bird was still up for it at her age? He'd always thought it was only men who didn't know when to call it a day. Still…why not? It certainly couldn't do him any harm.

"You're right," he said. "There is something else…but why don't we discuss it at my place?"

Dave…

Hugh, the landlord of the Regent, looked at his watch, and was surprised to find it had gone ten o'clock. He was surprised, because he had expected to see Dave by nine at the latest…but in the unexpected rush he'd forgotten all about time…and Dave.

Trish, Esther…

You don't get your name in lights for being a good father…or a good brother, come to that, and Trish knew how much she and Louise owed Oliver for staying behind in Norfolk to look after their parents while they went off to the States to pursue their careers. Not that he'd ever begrudged them their success, but perhaps it would have been nice if they'd done more to acknowledge his part in it. And that was what she'd been thinking about since the cards were put away.

"I've had an idea," she said to Esther now. "Did Tim ever consider writing his memoirs?"

"Not seriously, no," said Esther. "He was approached a couple of times, but he always said it was too soon. Why?"

"What about diaries…and letters?"

"What about them?"

"Did he keep them? I bet you've kept yours from him, haven't you?"

"Most of them, yes…"

"And his school reports, certificates…that sort of thing? Photographs…?"

"Yes, but…"

"Good…because the publishers are going to be falling over each other in the rush to tell his story now, and I think it would make sense to get in first."

"What, write it myself, you mean?"

"No, but I'm sure there are plenty of reputable writers out there who'd give their eye teeth for access to the material you've got. Make it exclusive access, and you could take your pick. You'd have to get Heather to co-operate of course, but I can't see her objecting if you told her why you were doing it. And you'd be doing it to make sure the true story was told – the whole story, including Oliver's part in it."

"A bit late for him," said Esther.

"Yes…well…better late than never, eh? Which reminds me. Have you managed to contact Harold yet?"

Louise, Gerry…

It was probably something to do with the sudden nature of Alfredo's success that the lighting in his restaurant had yet to be adapted to its new-found status, which didn't matter so much in the dining room itself, as the wall lights were dimmed and the tables lit by candles; but it was a ghastly sight that greeted Louise when she went to the 'ladies' to freshen up, while Gerry settled the bill – her own reflection in the mirror.

A crone in a party frock – that was what she saw – as opposed to the lightly-tanned sophisticate she'd spent hours getting ready, and it was a long walk back to the table, where Gerry was waiting to help her into her coat.

"Our taxi's here," he said.

"Look, I'm sorry, Gerry," she said. "But would you mind ordering another one?"

Simon…

Eleven o' clock, and still no sign of Alan at The Rondel – the house in Holland Park that Simon shared with Ronnie – not even a phone call. If Simon had put his mind to it, he might just have worked out that Alan didn't have his phone number, but as far as he was aware, he had no more reason to do that than he did to doubt Victor's word that Alan had run off with his wallet; so by eleven o' clock he had more or less given up hope. And then the phone did ring. But it was Gerry, wanting to know if he fancied popping round for an hour or two.

Knowing all too well what that meant, his first inclination was to say no, but having spent the last few hours coming to terms with a return to the state of affairs that had existed before last Friday, he decided that delaying it now, would only be a sop to false hope, so having asked Gerry to give him half an hour, he poured himself another large gin, and went upstairs to shower and change.

On the way over there, his taxi passed Canterbury Court, and he could see that the lights in Victor's flat were all off. Out drowning his sorrows probably, but over a temporary loss of face rather than a wallet full of cash, and it was highly unlikely that he would have risked further humiliation by going to the police. Victor often said things he didn't mean.

A few days ago, he had come up with the outrageous claim that Simon lacked self-esteem. Simon had been a bit miffed at the time – especially when Victor had walked out of the room without giving him a chance to put his own case – but he'd had to laugh this morning, when one of the girls at rehearsals had challenged the rest of the cast to answer a questionnaire she'd found in a magazine, under the heading: 'Living With Yourself – Your Partner and Your Self-Esteem'. It was a magazine Victor subscribed to, and almost certainly the inspiration behind his sweeping allegation, with questions like:

- ♦ Do you apologise more than you used to?
- ♦ Do you make excuses for your partner when he/she treats you badly?
- ♦ Do you regularly explain yourself without being asked to?
- ♦ Do you accept the blame to keep the peace?
- ♦ Is it becoming impossible for you to recall a conversation without feeling dissatisfied with your own contribution to it?

And so on.

The idea was that every 'yes' box ticked brought the reader a step lower in his or her own estimation – a lot of nonsense, of course, and beyond making him blush a bit, it hadn't bothered Simon unduly this morning, when his score had come out lowest of all. But Alan had been in the picture then.

Now, in the taxi on the way to Gerry's, having all but reconciled himself to a future with a man he didn't love, he was indulging himself in a little self-justification. What was self-esteem after all, if it didn't end up running off with your best friend's wallet? At least he knew where he stood with Ronnie.

Heather...

Heather climbed into bed disappointed. This morning she had taken it for granted that Gerry would be back by this evening, but he had phoned her an hour or so ago to say something had come up, and he'd be staying in town tonight, so not to expect him till morning.

Still, at least the spooky guy in the waistcoat had kept out of the way. Perhaps Gerry was right about him, after all.

Gerry, Simon...

Gerry greeted Simon with a kiss on the mouth, and then promptly started undressing him against the back of the front door as usual, only to discover Simon wasn't responding with his customary enthusiasm.

"What's up with you?" he said.

"Oh, I don't know," said Simon. "Guilt, I suppose."

"Guilt? Well, if it's Ronnie you're feeling guilty about, allow me to put your mind at rest."

"What do you mean?"

"Why do you think I phoned you in the first place, you silly sod?"

"Sorry, I'm not with you?"

"I'm not supposed to phone you at home, am I?"

"Oh, that... well, don't worry about it... Ronnie's at his mother's."

"Is he now? Funny... it didn't look like his mother I saw him with half an hour ago. Oh yes, and what's all this I hear about Ronnie and my late brother-in-law?"

Cassie...

The fact that I, personally, can't will a book to fall off a shelf, doesn't necessarily mean it can't be done.

This is what Cassie writes in her diary late on Wednesday night, and in its way it sums up her attitude to life, which is to try and look at every situation from more than one point of view.

Tonight's talk was about telekinesis, which put me in mind of a conversation I had with Harold a couple of weeks ago.
I caught him looking up a quote about moving mountains – the one from Gabriel's sermon in Shotgunning – and the question arose as to where Gabriel's powers came from. I said it wasn't where they came from that mattered, but what he did with them, and Harold suggested starting small...by sitting under a tree, and willing a leaf to fall into your hand, for instance. On Saturday afternoon, I followed him to the top field, where he sat down under the big horse chestnut in the corner.
It was during that same conversation that I told Harold I was going away with Larry, but I didn't say where to or when – just why – because even after thirty years of sleeping with a married man on a regular basis, I still feel the need to justify myself to someone, and as Harold is the only person who knows about me and Larry, it has to be him. Did I give him the details later? I don't think so, and yet on Saturday morning, after

I'd fallen asleep, having spent half the night looking out for him, he left me a note telling me he knew about Tim, and not to change my plans, as he wanted some time to himself. So how did he know I had plans to change...?

Yesterday some guy interrupted Larry's talk about out-of-body experiences, to tell him about someone he'd met on the astral plane – a character straight out of a Western, he said – and the minute Larry told me about it, a picture of Harold came into my mind – Harold dressed as Gabriel with his paranormal powers.

Steady, girl, you're letting your imagination run away with you...

Tonight's talk didn't go quite as smoothly as last night's, because a couple of hoorays from the hotel bar managed to infiltrate the Empress Suite, and insisted on Larry giving them a demo. He refused on the grounds that there were too many negative vibes in the room, but of course, that didn't satisfy them, and in the end he had to call security.

Two hours later, and he's here in bed beside me, sleeping like a man with nothing on his conscience. Or do I mean a man without a conscience at all?

Thursday, 23

Furze Cottage
Allingham Estate
Norfolk

10th March, 1951

Dearest Harold,

Of course we'd love to see you at Easter, especially Reg, who craves young company more than ever, without The Players to keep him occupied. And what with Oliver spending so much time up at the vicarage these days, and the girls away in America. He misses them terribly.
 I was going to offer you Trish's old room, but Oliver said he was sure you would rather stick with tradition and bunk in with him. Tradition, I said. You've only known each other five minutes. But of course what seems like five minutes to an old girl like me, turns out to be the best part of five years. Anyway, unless I hear otherwise, I'll make up the spare bed in Ollie's room.

> Let us know what time you'll be arriving, and one of us will meet you at the station.
>
> Much love,
> Tilly

Harold couldn't find anyone to cover his lunchtime shift on Saturday, so it was early evening by the time he arrived at Furze Cottage, where he was welcomed by Reg and Tilly, who explained that Oliver was up at the vicarage, helping Esther's father prepare for tomorrow's sunrise service; but they were sure he would be home soon.

When he did eventually appear, supper was ready, so it was bedtime before he got the chance to speak to Harold alone, and after lights out when he told him his news.

"I'm thinking of proposing to Esther," he said.

"Are you?" said Harold. "Well...good luck." And then for want of something more appropriate to add: "Have you told Reg yet?"

"It was his idea actually...that I should do it now, I mean. He doesn't think we should get married for another year or two, but he knows he's losing his marbles, and he's talking about signing everything over to me on my twenty-first. Reckons it'll be easier for Esther if I ask her while I'm still a relative pauper."

"And do you reckon that too?"

"Not really, no. But I'm going to ask her sometime, aren't I...? So if it makes him happy..."

The tradition in the village of May was to celebrate Easter in the meadow behind the church, from where the congregation could watch the sun rise over the river, before joining the vicar and his family for breakfast in the church hall. So Oliver was up and away before dawn, and the arrangement was that he would invite Esther back to the cottage for lunch.

Harold was awake when he left, and tempted to make his escape while the going was good, but manners got the better of him, and he was rewarded a couple of hours later, when he came downstairs to discover that Reg had had a restless night, and Tilly was letting him sleep in. A good excuse for a solitary walk around the estate.

He came back along the river bank, and was just about to turn for home when he came across Esther sitting alone on the so-called love seat Oliver had carved out of a fallen tree five summers ago.

"Hello, stranger," she said, when she saw him approaching. "I was just thinking about you."

"That's funny," he said. "We must have conjured each other up. Oliver not with you?"

"No, he went on ahead. He wanted a private word with Reg."

"Oh…right. We'll walk back together then, shall we?"

"That'd be nice."

On the way, Esther put her arm through his, and they fell silent for a while, but when the cottage loomed into view, she said:

"Oliver's asked me to marry him."

"Has he?" said Harold.

"You don't sound very surprised. Did you know?"

"Not exactly, no…but he did say he was thinking about it."

"And what did you say?"

"I wished him good luck, of course."

"I see…I'll say yes then, shall I?"

Trish, Esther, Louise…

It was with great relief all round that Trish and Esther sat down to breakfast with Louise on Thursday morning, after an unavailing twenty minutes or so on the cruel nature of fluorescent light, when she got home last night. Because there were two photographs side by side on the front page of today's *Telegraph* – one each of Louise and Gerry arriving at Alfredo's 'within minutes of each other' – and there was no getting away from the implication of the piece – or the fact that she looked every bit as stunning as he did.

"You always did take a good picture," said Trish, passing the paper back across the table.

"Do you think so?" said Louise. "Oh damn! Now I've gone and got butter all over it."

"Never mind," said Esther, trying hard not to smile. "I expect we can get another one."

"I saw that," said Louise.

"Saw what?" said Esther.

"The way you were looking at my dressing gown just then."

"I was not."

"Yes you were…and if that's the paperboy at the door, it's got nothing to do with me."

"Liar," said Trish, and then to Esther: "She was on the phone to the newsagent before the *Telegraph* hit the mat."

"Well," said Louise, getting up to answer the intercom. "I thought it might be nice to send Max a copy."

Belinda...

Belinda strode past Doctor Holman's receptionist and out into the street, where she'd left her car parked on a double yellow line. She was impatient to talk to Jack, and after a few frantic seconds scrabbling around in her handbag, she found her mobile at last, only to discover that it had run out of credits. There was a phone box on the other side of the road, but there was also a traffic warden working his way along the kerb towards her, and the last thing she needed now was a confrontation with him, so she thought better of it, and decided to wait until she got home. Which is why, when she did get around to making her call, she was in such a state, it didn't cross her mind to withhold her own number before dialling Jack's.

Heather...

Heather had spent the morning drinking coffee and reading magazines – watching breakfast television, unloading the dishwasher...in fact anything at all to try and convince herself that life was getting back to normal – apart from swimming.

   At eleven Gerry rang to say he was on his way back from town, so she went upstairs to shower, and then if there was still time she might stroll down to the village shop to stock up on a few basics.

Jack...

On his way over to meet Belinda at Nobby's flat, Jack tried to imagine what it could possibly be that was so important it couldn't wait until this afternoon. They had a matinee at three. And to phone him at home...

Fortunately though, there'd been no harm done there, as he'd managed to hang up a split second before Moira came into the room.

Heather...

While she was in her bedroom undressing, Heather caught sight of the photographs on the wall opposite the door – one each of her and Tim, taken soon after they got back from honeymoon. Gerry had remarked on them yesterday, when he came down for breakfast.

"I love the one of you," he'd said. "Poor Tim didn't stand a chance really, did he?"

Three years ago, at a party in Little Venice...

Having blagged their way in somehow, she and Gerry were talking about fame and its rewards, and the lengths each of them would be prepared to go to get what they wanted.

"Would you sleep with someone?" he said.

"No, I would not," she said.

"*I* would..."

And she laughed.

"No..." he said. "I mean anyone."

"What...*anyone*?"

"I think so, yes...if I thought it would get me what I wanted. A bit of blackmail, perhaps..."

"*Gerry!*"

"What do you want me to do...lie?"

"All right, then...what about murder?"

"Maybe...if I thought I'd get away with it."

And a couple of minutes later, Tim had walked up and introduced himself.

Back to the photographs, and yesterday Gerry had mentioned how uncomfortable he felt under Tim's gaze, now that he was dead. At the time Heather had been too preoccupied to take much notice, but this morning she finished undressing in the bathroom, and when she came downstairs some twenty minutes later, there was only one picture hanging on the wall in her bedroom. Tim's was lying face down on the bottom shelf of her wardrobe. She could always put it back in a day or two.

Jack, Belinda…

Jack could not have been less prepared for Belinda's news. In fact having recovered from the shock of her phoning him at home, he had managed to put the urgency in her voice out of his mind, and started to fantasise about what her naked body would look like in another month, say…or two. But he was destined never to see Belinda's naked body again – not even when it turned up on the mortuary slab in a few hours' time. That dubious privilege would fall to her husband.

"Old-fashioned," she was saying now, the blame game having ended in a stalemate. "That's what he called it, Jack…good old-fashioned syphilis. You'd have thought the man was giving me good news."

"Well," said Jack. "I don't suppose he meant it like that, did he? I mean he prob…"

"I know what he meant, Jack!" And then again with resignation: "I know what he meant…"

Heather, Nora...

The post office counter was in darkness when Heather wandered into the village shop after her stroll down from the Manor House. Nora was there though – Nora Johnson, who ran the shop with her husband, Wilf – putting the finishing touches to her new window display while it was quiet; and if her welcome was a little strained, it was anything but hostile. It was just that she was lost for words, as anyone might be in the presence of the recently bereaved. And her dilemma was made worse by the fact that, apart from Heather herself, she was probably the last person to have seen Tim alive. He had called into the shop on the very evening he died – to buy a packet of aspirins.

Heather decided to make things easier for her.

"I just wanted to thank you," she said.

"To thank me...?" said Nora.

"Yes...for all the support you've given us over the years. Particularly Tim. He often said how much it meant to him to be able to walk in here and be treated like a normal human being, instead of being gawped at like some exhibit at the zoo."

"Well...it's nice of you to say so. We were all very fond of him, you know."

"I know..."

A phone started ringing in the passage behind the shop, and having insisted on Nora answering it, Heather grabbed a wire basket from the stack beside the check-out counter, and headed for the fresh produce section. But before she could reach it, she caught sight of her reflection in the door of the drinks cabinet. And over her shoulder...a face at the window.

Belinda...

Belinda was sitting behind the wheel of her car – on the third floor of the multi-storey car park next to the theatre. She had been there for more than an hour now – staring at a concrete wall covered in graffiti – and she could not have felt more alone.

Snatches of her conversation with Doctor Holman kept coming back to her. Good old-fashioned syphilis, he'd called it, this complaint of hers. She'd known what he meant, of course, but in the circumstances that was hardly a comfort to her.

"What about the baby?" she'd said. "Will it be all right?"

"I don't see why not," he'd said. "You see, while we're treating you, we'll be treating the baby too."

But was he right? He was awfully old, Doctor Holman, and a bit of a dinosaur too, as the breezy manner in which he'd delivered Belinda's news had illustrated. That had been a clumsy attempt to show her how non-judgmental he was. But Belinda had been going to him since she was a little girl, and it was going to take a lot more than one ill-considered attack of chumminess to persuade her he'd moved with the times. So what if his methods were locked in the past too? Or his understanding of the long-term effects of a disease? What if the baby turned out to have been irreparably damaged?

Belinda did wonder if she ought to enquire about

getting rid of it, just in case, but she soon put that idea out of her mind. Rodney knew about it now, and Rodney would never forgive her if she had an abortion without good reason. Good reason…

Being the man he was, Doctor Holman had presumed it was Rod who had infected Belinda rather than the other way round, and insisted that once it was confirmed, he was going to have to inform everyone he had been in sexual contact with for the past six months or more. But how was she going to tell him that, when it was his proud boast that he hadn't so much as looked at another woman since the day they met. No, it was going to have to be the truth…or nothing.

Gerry, Heather…

Gerry was already in possession of the facts, if not the detail, by the time Wilf Johnson dropped Heather off at the cottage. And it was the second time she had fainted in less than a week.

"So, what happened?" he said.

"Well," said Heather. "I was on my own in the shop, when I saw this guy staring at me through the window."

"What…the dude in the waistcoat?"

"That was what I thought, yes…until the next thing I knew I was waking up on a settee in the back room, and he and Wilf were standing over me like a couple of expectant fathers. He was just a delivery man."

Jack, Belinda...

It seems that the show really must go on, because at four-fifteen on Thursday afternoon, Jack and Belinda were in the middle of the sketch that opened the second half of *A Czech in the Post*, while several coach loads of OAPs looked on in bewilderment. Ironic that, as the sketch was called 'George and Gracie', and was based on an act Olivia Nuttall had seen on television as a child. It had been history even then – an ancient black and white recording of a live stage performance – but this lot were old enough to have been in the audience.

"Have you met Bill?" Jack was saying.

"Who's Bill?" said Belinda.

"The man who owns this place."

"No, I don't believe I have. Have you?"

"Oh yes, he's a good friend. We're both Rotarians, actually."

"Are you? That's a coincidence. I'm going there for my holidays."

"Where?"

"Rotaria."

Gerry, Heather...

"Here, get this down you," said Gerry, handing Heather a cup of coffee.

"Thanks," said Heather.

"Do you want a brandy with it?"

"No...I'm fine for the moment, thanks."

"What do you mean, for the moment? You're not planning on staying, are you?"

But she could tell he was only joking.

"Would you mind?" she said.

"No, of course not. I was going to suggest it, anyway. You see, apart from anything else, I think it's about time you and I sat down and had a nice long chat."

Simon, Polly, Alan…

Simon's director – the man whose job it was to shape him into a convincing Buster Sergeant for this, the latest adaptation of *Naval Reserve* – was called Ernest Payne, and the idea had always been that at the end of each afternoon session, he would hold court at a pub near the rehearsal studio, for any members of the cast who cared to join him. Most had taken up the offer yesterday, and would again today, as there was an uneasy feeling, especially among the least confident in their ranks, that it was expected of them, and might somehow work against them if they failed to show up. Others just went along for the free drink.

Polly Hampton fell into the latter category, but she did have some sympathy for her less experienced colleagues.

"You look tired," she said to Simon, when they found themselves stranded on the nearside kerb together, having been cut off from the others by a sudden surge of traffic.

"I am," he said. "In fact, to tell you the truth, I'm absolutely shattered."

"What you need is a damn good massage," said Polly. "And if I didn't think I was totally wasting my time, I'd…aah, look…that poor lad's been sitting there since nine o' clock this morning."

"Which poor lad?"

But as he said it, Simon saw Alan, sitting on his haversack in the doorway opposite – and he was fast asleep.

Inside the pub the rest of the cast were arranging themselves around the table in the window, while Ernest Payne settled to the task of reminding them of his pedigree.

"Now as you all know," he was saying. "I came to this project a complete Buster Sergeant virgin..."

"Just give me a minute, will you?" said Simon to Polly.

"Where are you going?" said Polly.

"Got to sort something out," said Simon, nipping between cars.

"...But I had studied the script, of course," said Ernest Payne to his enraptured audience. "And my one reservation about taking it on was to do with the relationship between Buster and his young friend Robbo. I mean, was it really credible that just a few hours in the company of a man he'd known for less than a week could change the course of Buster's life so drastically...?"

"Well, of course it was," said Alan with a beatific smile; and then opening his eyes and seeing Simon: "I think Vic's on to us."

Heather, Gerry...

"So," said Heather, when Gerry finally emerged from the spare bedroom, which doubled as his personal gym. "What was it you wanted to chat about?"

"Tim, of course," he said, disappearing into the kitchen. And then reappearing seconds later with a bottle and two glasses: "Pizza all right for dinner, by the way?"

"Yes, fine. So...what about him?"

"Well, there's his will, for a start. I don't suppose I get a mention, do I?"

"I've no idea."

"Liar."

"No, seriously, I haven't. His solicitor's got it, and according to Esther he's not due back off holiday till next week. I suppose I could have asked one of his underlings to dig it out, but I thought that might look a bit…hasty…"

"Oh well, I won't hold my breath. In fact, when I come to think about it, he was always going to be worth more to me alive than dead."

"How do you mean?"

"Just this little ongoing arrangement I had. Did he ever used to talk about Vic at all?"

"Not much, no…why?"

"Nothing about why he signed up with him in the first place?"

"I thought *you* put them on to each other?"

"I did…but there was a bit more to it than that."

"Was there?"

"Yes. Vic's agency needed a bit of a kick start, you see, and I came up with this idea that with someone like Tim on his books, he might make a name for himself."

"Right…"

"So I cooked up this little scheme to persuade him to do it. Tim, I mean. I knew he wouldn't leave the Delaneys for no good reason, but if it was to protect my reputation, he might think twice. So I told him Vic had something on me."

"What sort of thing?"

"A video…and I don't mean the sort of video you're

likely to find on the shelf of your local Woolies either."

But to Gerry's slight disappointment, Heather was more puzzled than shocked.

"And did it exist, this video?"

"Oh yes...I gave it to Vic myself. In fact, I had it made specially, the idea being that if Tim didn't jump at the chance of joining his stable, he could put pressure on him by threatening to show it to you. We worked out this yarn about it being the only copy left after the rest had been destroyed in a fire...something like that anyway..."

"And did Tim fall for it?"

"It never got that far apparently, because Vic decided to try the softly softly approach first, and no sooner had he told Tim I owed him some sort of favour, than Tim was signing on the dotted line, no questions asked. Talk about a result..."

"Yes...for Vic. But what did you get out of it?"

"A percentage of the business."

"And what happened to the video?"

"Vic's still got it. He kept it as an insurance against Tim changing his mind."

"And you're happy about that, are you?"

"Oh yes. I've always had far more on Vic than he's ever had on me."

"Well, maybe...but I still think I'd ask for it back if I were you. I mean, with Tim out of the picture, it's not as if it's serving any useful purpose, is it?"

"That's what you think," said Gerry, with a knowing grin...and then almost as an afterthought: "Do you know what I think?"

"No...what?"

"I think you killed your husband. Now then, three different cheeses, or bacon and mushroom?"

Jack, Olivia…

Jack was beginning to wonder if this day was ever going to end. Matinee days normally provided him with a legitimate excuse to spend some time with Belinda between shows, but this afternoon she had disappeared the moment the three o' clock performance was over, and then failed to return for the evening call, leaving him to play his reluctant part, while Olivia Nuttall played hers.

Tomorrow, when the tragic truth was splashed across the tabloids, those present would be able to boast to their friends about how they'd been in at the kill, so to speak. Some would wish that Belinda had managed to hold on just a little bit longer, but the overall consensus among those who were able to make the comparison, would be that Ms Nuttall had more than made up for any inconvenience, particularly when it came to her impression of Gracie Allen.

"No, no, Gracie," Jack was saying now. "We don't *come* from Rotaria. We're members of the Rotary Club."

"Oh, I see. Who comes from Rotaria, then?"

"No one. There's no such place."

"Isn't there? So how come I'm going there on holiday?"

"You can't be. You're probably thinking of Rotorua."

"Oh no, I remember now. It's Albania."

"Albania? But that doesn't even begin with an R."

"No, I know…but Ruthie does."

"And who, pray, is Ruthie?"

"My best friend. Haven't you met her?"

"No, I don't believe I have. She's from Albania, is she?"

"No, silly…she's a member of the Albany Club."

Heather, Gerry…

So, at last Heather was telling Gerry her story – just as she'd always known she would – and he was taking it as calmly as he'd taken her decision about the topping on her pizza.

She'd been thinking about killing Tim for ages, she said. Strange then, that when she'd done it, it had been more or less on a whim. The two of them had been preparing for a swim, when she'd complained of a headache. There were no aspirins in the house – or so she'd told him – and sure enough, Tim had offered to go into the village to buy some. Sealing his fate, he had slipped his trousers on over his swimming trunks, and before she'd had time to reconsider, he'd gone.

There were half a dozen sun loungers stacked against the wall of the pool house. To move one would be to commit herself to the next stage of her plan, which she did, placing its foot a matter of inches away from the pool's edge, before switching off the light and lying down to wait.

Tim returned to a twilit pool house. He called out to her, and she answered him. Yes, she was all right, thanks. It was just this headache, and the light had been so bright. She was only lying down for a minute.

Tim fetched a glass of water from the changing room, and tipped a couple of aspirins out of the packet. Then he came and sat on the end of Heather's lounger, and offered her the pills from his open palm.

She sat up, and the bed tilted. Tim felt his balance going, and even as he struggled to regain it – even as a peal of involuntary laughter rose in his throat – Heather was lunging out at him with her foot, and he was falling backwards into the deep end.

He wasn't a swimmer, poor Tim – Heather herself had only recently insisted on giving him lessons – and he had swallowed a lot of water, before the buoyancy in his clothes brought him to the surface for the first time. But it was those same clothes that provided Heather with the means for pulling him under again, for she was in the water now too, tugging at the cuffs of his trousers, dragging him down to the bottom of the pool, where she hoped her own preparedness, skill and staying power would combine with the elements of surprise, inexperience and sheer panic in her husband, to help her outlast him in the struggle for air.

He didn't give up straight away, but his flailing arms had grown tired long seconds before he realised he was being held under, by which time he was too weak even to try and reach down to free himself. Instinctively he kicked out, but his legs were heavy and he could barely drag his shoes through the water – and all the time Heather held on.

Finally she had to come up, and when she did Tim came up too. But he was almost gone now, and from her position behind him, it was a simple matter of placing one flat palm against the nape of his neck, the other on his forehead, and tilting his head back under the water, until the spark of recognition vanished from his disbelieving eyes.

When it was all over, she went to the pool house door and locked it from the inside. Then, hastily but calmly, she returned to the pool and undressed Tim down to his swimming trunks, after which she crossed to the changing room, and showered and dressed, before placing the lounger back on its stack against the wall. After that, she gathered up her swimming costume, together with Tim's wet clothes, used her own towel to mop up the puddle they'd left, and finally, switched on the light to survey the scene of the crime. Her riskiest moment – but the pool house was well hidden from the road – and it only took a second or two to satisfy herself that everything was in its proper place. Then she switched the light back off and left.

Once inside the house, she put Tim's clothes and her own swimming things into the washing machine, and then flushed the remaining aspirins from the old packet down the lavatory. Just as well Tim had taken her word on having run out. She chucked the empty packet in the bin, and then, while the washing machine went through its motions, she dried her hair before lying on her bed, until she heard the machine go into its final spin.

Into the tumble drier went the evidence – she even ironed it afterwards – and once it was returned to its original pristine condition – Tim had always been an immaculate dresser – she made one final journey to the pool house, where, with barely a glance at the body floating face down in the water, she made her way directly to the changing room, and deposited Tim's clothes. Now she was ready to play out the tragedy as she'd tell it, and in the unlikely event that Nora Johnson or anyone else who had seen Tim in the village earlier was called upon to describe how he'd been dressed, their stories would tally with the actual evidence – apart from the shoes, of course. Heather had had to take a chance there, by replacing the ones that had been soaked in the pool with a similar pair she'd found in Tim's wardrobe afterwards. But then nothing is ever a hundred per cent, is it?

"No, it's not," said Gerry, when she'd finished her story. "Although I think it's highly unlikely that you'll be undone by a pair of chlorinated shoes. What intrigues me, though, is what you would have done if something else had gone wrong…something basic like…well, say, for instance, Tim hadn't sat on the end of the lounger?"

"But I knew he would," said Heather. "I arranged it that way."

"Yes, but just say he hadn't?"

"Well, I'd have taken the aspirins, and gone to bed," she said. "…And tried again another day."

Esther, Trish, Louise…

"It was the most disgusting thing I have ever seen," said Esther. "But I couldn't bring myself to confront him about it, so I just swept up the pieces, put Ben on his lead, and walked out of the house. And that was the last I saw of him."

"So, what are you going to do now?" said Trish.

"I don't know…ask him for a divorce, I suppose."

"And do you think he'll agree?"

"He will if the money's right."

"I don't see why *you* should have to pay *him*," said Louise.

"No, nor do I," said Esther. "But on the other hand, I'm not really in the right frame of mind for a battle at the moment. I'd rather just pay up and have done with it. I can't say I'm looking forward to going back, though."

"I wouldn't mind a little trip down to Brighton," said Trish. "What do you think, Lou? We could both go, couldn't we? A nice change of scenery for us…a bit of moral support for Esther?"

"No, it's a lovely thought," said Esther. "But not this time, if you don't mind."

"Why not?" said Louise. "When are you thinking of going?"

"Tomorrow," said Esther.

"Tomorrow! Well, I suppose we…oh, no, hang on, we can't. I've just remembered. We've been invited out tomorrow night."

"Have we?" said Trish.

"Yes…I don't suppose you remember a chap called Meredith Parker, do you?"

"Meredith Parker!" said Trish. "Well…I never thought I'd hear that name again. What have we been invited to do…put flowers on his grave?"

Esther snorted, and Louise said:

"Aah, don't be like that, darling. He's appearing in cabaret, actually, and…"

"Cabaret!" said Trish. "What doing, for God's sake? Balancing plates on the end of his…?"

"Trish!"

Esther snorted again, and Trish said:

"Well, I'm sorry, Lou, but you don't know the half of it. Do you know what that old fool did to me once?"

"No…what?"

"He only exposed himself to me, that's all."

"What? Meredith Parker did? When?"

"When you were making that film with him. What was it called again? *Banderolos*? *Bandolieros*?"

"*Banderilleros*," said Louise. "And they wondered why it bombed. But that must have been the best part of thirty years ago, wasn't it?"

"So…what difference does that make?"

"All right…keep your shirt on. I was just wondering why you didn't say anything at the time, that's all."

"Because I knew what you'd do if I did, that's why. And believe it or not, he was quite a big shot back then."

"Yes…I know. So, go on then…what exactly did he do?"

"Well…I was sitting in your trailer waiting for you, when suddenly I heard a strange sound behind me…and when I looked round, there it was – Meredith Parker's you-know-what – poking through the fly curtain…with a doughnut on it."

"How did you know it was him?" said Louise, and Esther took a fit of the giggles.

"Well, you don't think I just left it at that, do you?" said Trish indignantly. "I said, 'Who's there?' and when he didn't answer, I told him if he didn't remove it immediately, I'd take a big stick to it…something like that anyway…"

"And did he…?" said Louise. "Remove it, I mean?"

"Well yes. He made a run for it, actually…but not before the doughnut fell off."

"So, how *did* you know it was him?"

"Because when he bent down to pick it up, his face came through the curtain."

"Oh, I see," said Louise, with a chuckle. "Well, that's a relief, anyway."

"Why?"

"Well, for a minute there, I had visions of you as a sort of latter day Prince Charming, scouring the lot to see which man it fitted."

Gerry, Heather

"I wouldn't go as far as to say I was envious," said Gerry, "but I've often wondered what it would be like to kill someone."

"Have you?" said Heather. "Well, don't hold your breath, but you might find out before long…"

"What do you mean?"

"…If the guy in the waistcoat shows up again. I think he might know."

"About Tim, you mean? How?"

"I'm not sure. Perhaps he saw me."

Gerry thought about this for a moment, and then said:

"No…if he'd seen you, he'd have turned you in by now."

"Not if he was intending to blackmail me, he wouldn't…and I don't think I could handle that."

"Really…? Well, oddly enough, I don't think I could handle life in Parkhurst…so we'd better just hope you're wrong, hadn't we?"

Polly…

If you had asked Polly Hampton to sum up her philosophy in one phrase, she would have said, 'Live and let live.' That was on Tuesday. Had you put the question a different way, or asked it on a different day, she might have told you she was 'a people person' or 'a doggy person', or that she was a feminist, or that she wasn't.

She sometimes said she believed in calling a spade a spade, and that she was not a woman to be dictated to, and that she didn't suffer fools gladly. On the other hand, she always put her coat on to answer the front door, in case it was a Jehovah's Witness, and she could say she was on her way out, but she wouldn't cross a gypsy, and she still thought of God as a man with a white beard. In other words, she was every bit as rational as the rest of the company.

It had never crossed her mind to consider the rights and wrongs of Simon's story – and even if it had, it wouldn't have made any difference. Had she ever met Ronnie – or at a push, even his mother – she might have been persuaded to see things from another point of view; but it was Simon she had befriended – and as a consequence, Alan – and if there was one thing she cherished above all else, it was friendship.

She could hear the pair of them snoring in her spare bedroom now – hardly surprising after the extraordinary exchange of energy she had witnessed in the street this afternoon – and whatever it was they were going to have to face tomorrow, they would be far better prepared for it after eight hours in a comfortable bed and a good hearty breakfast.

Rodney…

Rodney was just about to listen to his telephone messages, when he spotted a policeman walking up the front path; and there was another one sitting behind the wheel of a panda car outside. They must have followed him.

Well, perhaps he had been gunning it a bit on the way home. But he'd also had a few beers after his workout tonight, and he was sure he'd heard tales of people being breathalysed in their houses, so to be on the safe side, when he did hear the doorbell ring, he poured himself a large scotch and soda before he answered it.

"Mr Lucas?" said the policeman, when he opened the door.

"No," said Rodney, taking a generous swig from his glass.

"Oh, I'm sorry," said the policeman. "Would it be possible to speak to him then please?"

"Not really," said Rodney, taking another swig. "There's no one of that name living here."

"Isn't there?" said the policeman. "That's odd. This is definitely the address I was given."

"There's a Mr Davis that lives here," said Rodney helpfully. "Married to some actress called Lucas, if I'm not mistaken. I wonder if it's him you're looking for?"

"Yes, that'll be the one," said the policeman. "Can I speak to him then…please?"

"You're speaking to him."

"I'm…you mean you're Mr Davis?"

"That's right."

"And you're married to Belinda Lucas?"

"Right again."

"Aah…" eyeing the glass uneasily. "Well in that case, do you mind if I come in? I'm afraid I've got some bad news for you."

Gerry, Heather…

"I've got to go up to town again in the morning," said Gerry.

"Oh…have you?" said Heather.

"Yes. Why, it's not a problem, is it?"

"Not really, no. I just don't like being left on my own at the moment, that's all."

"Well, you won't be for long…I promise. I take it you are staying the night?"

"Do you mind?"

"No, of course not. And then you can help yourself to what you want out of the fridge in the morning, and I'll drop you off at the house on my way to the station. Oh, and I've done those tapes for you too, so you'll have something to occupy yourself with until I phone you."

"Aren't you coming back then?"

"Maybe…maybe not. Just make sure you're there when I phone, that's all."

"Gerry…what are you up to?"

"One o' clock…all right?"

Victor…

Victor got a taxi home, having had his car keys confiscated by the manager of the pub next door to the Bear and

Whippet, after getting himself involved in a game of Jack the Ripper with a group of young students on a sightseeing tour.

The game consisted of half a dozen players taking it in turns to deal a pack of cards – face up – until all the jacks were out. First jack chose a drink – a double Pernod and Tia Maria, for instance, or a Crème de Menthe, port and banana liqueur cocktail – in other words, any alcoholic concoction at all, as long as it was vile to drink and cost a bomb. Second jack paid for it, jack number three drank it, and jack number four…now what was it jack number four did again? Victor wasn't sure, although he did vaguely remember suggesting what one number four might quite like to do, and it had only been the intervention of a pretty hefty bouncer that had saved him from the sort of beating he occasionally paid to witness.

Once in the sanctuary of his own living room, he poured himself a proper drink, and sat down on the floor in front of the settee, on which just forty-eight hours earlier he had smoked his first joint.

He couldn't remember much about that either, to be honest – only that the first few drags hadn't seemed to have any effect at all. Next thing, though, he'd been waking up on the settee where Alan had left him, so perhaps someone had known what he was doing…crafty fucker…or was that all some people ever got out of it – a good night's sleep? Victor had heard that it affected different people in different ways.

Leaning over to put his glass on the coffee table, he noticed an ashtray on the floor next to one of the armchairs, and alongside it on the carpet, a half-smoked joint and a box of matches. Five minutes later, having taken just one cautious pull on the strongest spliff Alan had ever rolled, he was lying on his back, waiting for something to happen – but nothing did. So he decided to have another go. Trouble was, that when he tried to sit up, he couldn't; and when he tried to roll over on to his stomach, he couldn't do that either – in fact, the effort made him feel quite nauseous. So he stayed where he was, and that was where his cleaning lady would find him when she came in on Monday morning – lying on his back, staring up at the ceiling, the vomit around his mouth having dried to a crust – because there was an unwritten rule in Canterbury Court, that the residents kept themselves to themselves.

Cassie...

It was dark by the time the taxi dropped Cassie off at the main gate. She had spent the afternoon in Tunbridge Wells, the idea being that if she and Larry arrived back at the Foundation separately and hours apart, they were less likely to arouse suspicion. Larry's idea, of course, and how well it appeared to have worked, because when Cassie passed the farmhouse there was a dinner party going on inside, and Larry was so at home in the part he was playing, that the last three days might never have happened.

This mattered, not least because there was only one path between the main gate and Cassie's caravan – a path that Larry must have realised she'd be taking some time this evening – and yet he hadn't even bothered to draw the curtains.

When she turned into the clearing, she saw that Harold's curtains were open too, and the light above his desk was switched on, but by now she'd lost her appetite for conversation, so she crept past his door and made her way to her own.

Friday, 24

Furze Cottage
Allingham Estate
Norfolk

29th July, 1968

Dear Harold,

I thought you might like this photo of your future godson, Timothy. He is dying to meet you, and says you can call him Tim, as long as you promise to take your role seriously.

Write to him regularly (he can practically read already), and visit him as often as you can. Talk to him, listen to him — make him happy just by being there. Love him.

I know he will love you. He is his mother's son.

Esther

At the age of thirty-seven Harold Masters was a star, and the trappings of his success included homes on both sides of the Atlantic, a collection of classic cars and an offhand way with women that seemed to rob them of their sanity. What he lacked was a desire for more of the same…a purpose, a soul mate, a reason for living.

He had no faith. When it came to filling in forms he still wrote C of E, but, unlike Oliver, who credited God with everything from his inherited fortune to the birth of his only child after fourteen years of daily prayer, Harold grew more sceptical with every reward life threw his way.

It didn't help matters that he was less than convinced by the spiritual alternatives a lot of his fellow entertainers were turning to, and even at his lowest ebb, he would still rather have negotiated the price of absolution with a certain Norfolk vicar than the Maharishi Mahesh Yogi. But it was no good. Christian, Buddhist, Muslim, Hindu – as far as Harold was concerned, the only undeniable truth was that more people had to be wrong than were right. Still, he envied Oliver his certainty. And Oliver had Esther too.

Oliver had Esther. Esther had a son. And Harold had a new car.

August, 1968, and he was on his way to Norfolk in the Daimler DS420, which had been waiting for him in Southampton when he docked the day before. Baby Tim was being christened the following morning, and Oliver and Esther had asked Harold to be one of his godparents; so he was planning to stay the night, while somehow wishing he had an excuse to delay his arrival.

He took a wrong turning, and came across a young

couple, trying to hitch a lift in a road that led nowhere. Runaways, was his first thought, and they looked so bedraggled he was tempted not to stop; but his good nature got the better of him, when the boy managed to catch his eye.

The boy. He must have been the best part of thirty himself, and his wife couldn't have been much younger, because the first thing they mentioned was the fact that they had a teenage daughter, who was going to be so, so jealous when she found out who'd picked them up. Apparently she had a life-sized picture of Harold on the wall above her bed. They were on their way home to her now, and were sorry if they stank, but they'd just been to a pop festival in the Isle of Wight.

They came from California, but for the last thirteen years they'd lived in a caravan on a farm complex in Kent, which, bearing in mind their daughter's age, made Harold wonder if they were one-time runaways after all. But there was more to it than that.

The farm had been bought out just after the Second World War, by a small group of conscientious objectors and their sympathisers, and despite strong local objection it had gone on to become a thriving community, dedicated to the principles of love, peace and spiritual well-being. That was how Luke described it, anyway, and Harold wasn't inclined to argue, particularly when he heard how Luke and Jenny came to be living there.

They had read about the place in a magazine article, headed 'The Calumet Foundation – Conchies Fight On'. It was dated January, 1954, and was about the continuing opposition the community faced from its neighbours.

Damage to their property, daily taunts, the constant threat of violence – Luke and Jenny had been so affected by the injustice of the way these peace-loving people were still being treated so long after the war, they'd decided to come over and offer their support. Thirteen years later they were still there.

Harold went a little bit out of his way to drop them off, and then, when they'd gone, he looked at the dirty marks on his upholstery, and made up his mind. With *Shotgunning* in the can, he was due a break anyway, and he could always think again if things didn't work out.

Esther…

How things might have worked out? This is what Esther is thinking about, as she gets ready for the lonely journey back to Brighton. How things might have worked out, if Reg had lived long enough to see his grandson christened. Or Ma…or even Tilly. Would Harold have turned his back on them too? Because that was what Oliver had accused him of doing – turning his back on his responsibilities as Timothy's godfather – and he'd used it as an excuse for refusing to visit Calumet. But Esther wondered now if there'd been more to it than that. Because he'd never tried to stop her going.

She was in no doubt at all that he had trusted her implicitly, and even after fourteen years of trying without success, there had never been any question of Tim's conception being anything other than the miracle it was; but perhaps, like Cassie, Oliver had recognised something vital in Esther's friendship with Harold – something he knew he didn't have the power to overcome – and it was only by distancing himself from it that he'd been able to continue to pretend it didn't exist.

How might things have worked out if Oliver had been more sure of himself? Esther remembers the first time she visited Calumet, when Harold opened his caravan door to find her standing there, with Tim in her arms.

"I've brought your godson to visit you," she said, and the look of delight that spread across his face lives on in her memory, the way it does in Cassie's. But if Oliver had been there, would that look have been the same?

All Esther knows for certain is that for the rest of his life her beloved son took as much pleasure in Harold's company as Harold did in his.

Gerry, Heather…

It was nine o' clock when Gerry dropped Heather off at the Manor House.

"Right then," he said, when she leaned into the car to kiss him. "Got everything?"

"Yes thanks."

"Good. I'll phone you later, then."

"Right."

"One o' clock…don't forget."

"I won't."

"You will be in, won't you?"

"Gerry…"

"Sorry. I'll speak to you later then…oh, what about the tapes?"

"What about them?"

"You did remember to pick them up, didn't you?"

The tapes he was referring to were recordings he'd made of a couple of Frank Cordino CDs he'd bought a few weeks ago. According to Gerry, Cordino was the best thing to have come out of New Jersey since Ol' Blue Eyes himself, and he'd been promising Heather copies of the CDs since the first day she heard them. Not that she'd ever pressed him for them. If music was as intrinsic to her domestic life as the wallpaper on her walls, she also paid it about as much attention; but she did appreciate the fact that Gerry had gone to the trouble of making them, and yes, she had remembered to bring them with her, which she demonstrated now, by waving them under his nose.

"Excellent," he said. "And you promise to play them this morning?"

"If you want me to, yes. But why's it so important."

"Never mind…just do it."

And he drove off.

Simon, Alan…

Where to start? That was the burning question facing Simon and Alan when they sat down to breakfast at Polly Hampton's table on Friday morning. Where to start? Not to mention when? And how?

How do you tell your partner you're leaving him after ten years? Or your mother that you've been checking out the gay scene in London for the past week, when you were supposed to have been camping in the Lake District with your school friends?

It occurred to Simon that, from his point of view, it

might be easier not to bring Alan into the argument at all. He was pretty sure Ronnie had been cheating on him, after all, so why not just say he was leaving because of that? On the other hand, the only reason he knew Ronnie hadn't been at his mother's on Wednesday night was because he himself hadn't been where he was supposed to be either – and besides, in his own grubby way, he'd been cheating on Ronnie since the day he met him. So what then? The truth?

As far as Alan was concerned that was what it was going to have to be from now on, despite what he believed it would mean to his mum. In her eyes he would be condemning himself to an eternity of hellfire, but he'd spent enough years indulging her whims, and there was someone else to consider now, so she was just going to have to accept him for what he was – or not.

Heather...

It was half past nine when Heather remembered the tapes. She'd been sitting in her favourite armchair going through her post – the usual mixed bag of fan mail, bills, circulars and letters of condolence – when for no particular reason she glanced through the open door, and spotted her bag lying on the hall table where she'd left it when she came in. The tapes were peeping out of it. Perhaps she should put one on now.

According to Gerry's index, 'If Only He Knew' was the opening song on side one of the tape he had dubbed 'Cordino Blue'; but a quick glance down the running order of 'Cordino Too' revealed that it was listed again towards the end of tape two – a later recording of the same song presumably. The second tape started with 'The World At My Feet' – a particular favourite of Frank's, apparently – so she put that one on, and went back to her post.

There was a touching card from Douglas McIntyre – the man Tim had commissioned to take the photographs hanging on the bedroom wall. Or at least one of them was still hanging there. The one of Tim was in the wardrobe, where she'd put it yesterday. But wouldn't that seem odd to anyone who went in there – like her cleaner, for instance, who was due in tomorrow morning? Better put it back.

The sound system in the Manor House had pairs of auxiliary speakers in all the main rooms, and these were controlled by a row of buttons on the main console in the living room. So Heather went over and pressed the button marked BEDROOM ONE, and then ran upstairs.

By the time she came back down, the first tape had come to an end, so she went to turn it over. But before she could press the PLAY switch, she remembered the carrier bag full of food she had brought back from Gerry's – bread, cold sausages, cheese and a pint of milk wrapped in newspaper, to keep everything else dry. It should have gone into the fridge the minute she came in. But she had no recollection of going anywhere near the fridge, so, forgetting all about the tapes, she went back into the hall.

The bag was propped up against the umbrella stand inside the front door, where she'd put it down for a moment while she gathered up her post. But no harm done. The newspaper had done its job, and the perishables were still dry, so she took the bag through to the kitchen to unpack.

It was while she was peeling the newspaper off the milk, that she noticed the date at the top of the page – Friday, 17 – and further down – that evening's television listings. One particular item caught her eye:

> **Film: Shotgunning (1968)**. Preacher, Gabriel Jones, uses paranormal powers to wreak vengeance on unrepentant members of his flock.
> Western, starring Harold Masters. (32733) *****

It was the film Tim had been talking about only hours before he died. He was going to tape it, he said, because he hadn't seen it for years, and it was the last thing Harold had done before quitting the business for good. Heather had never met Harold, but she'd heard enough about him to know he was the last person she would want to meet now.

A one-time Hollywood heartthrob, Harold had spent the last thirty years living in a commune somewhere near Tunbridge Wells. *'A small self-contained community of some hundred or so souls, dedicated to inner peace through hard physical work and meditation'* – that was how the residents of the Calumet Foundation described themselves in the brochures they sent out to advertise their workshops. Tim had shown her one soon after they met. But Gerry had insisted on seeing it too, and Gerry had no patience for New Agers and their pretensions.

"You don't actually believe all that crap, do you?" he'd said to Tim after reading it. But far from taking offence, Tim had given the question some thought before answering:

"To be honest, Gerry, I don't know what to believe, and

from what he tells me, I don't think Harold does either. I mean, they couldn't be a more welcoming bunch if they tried, but my problem's always been with the way they look at you when they're talking to you. Their eyes are so unnaturally wide open, you could almost be forgiven for thinking they'd been hypnotised or drugged or something. But it's not that. Or at least I don't think it is. I think it's more to do with their belief that a steady gaze is a sincere one, so by holding you in theirs, so to speak, they're killing two birds with one stone – demonstrating their own sincerity, and challenging yours at the same time. It can be quite unnerving."

It was the closest Tim had ever come to criticising Calumet, and he certainly hadn't meant it as a warning, but even at that early stage in the relationship Heather had taken it as one, and she had resolved there and then to avoid Harold Masters at all costs. Fortunately for her, Harold had played right into her hands by not coming to her wedding – he never left Calumet – and since then she had always made sure she was too busy to accompany Tim when he went there. Just as well the way things had turned out.

Still, it was a bit of a coincidence that one of his films had been on television the day his godson died. She went up to Tim's den.

It was still there in his video recorder, where he'd set it up last Friday. Heather never used the television in Tim's den, and she hadn't paid it any attention on the couple of occasions she'd visited the room during the past week – the little red light, which indicated that the machine had not been switched on since it had last been set up to record.

She switched it on now, pressed the rewind button on the remote – and waited.

There was a magazine lying open on the arm of the chair where the remote had been. It was dated Sunday, 12, and it carried all the television listings for the following week. It was open at last Friday's page, but it wasn't the programme details that grabbed Heather's attention. It was a photograph publicising the late night film, starring Harold Masters as Gabriel Jones – a face staring out from under a tilted bowler.

It was the face that had been haunting Heather all week – since Saturday morning, when she'd spotted the old man in the lane outside her bedroom window. No wonder he'd seemed familiar. Strange though, that somewhere in the house there was an album full of photographs of Harold, which Tim had taken great delight in showing her from time to time – Harold in his cinematic heyday and at every stage of his friendship with Tim's parents; Harold nursing his newly-christened godson on the steps of the church; Harold with his neighbour, Cassie, in the grounds of his precious Calumet; in fact Harold from every conceivable angle – except this one. Heather had never seen this photograph before, and it was quite different from all the others. It was him all right – she could see that now – but his expression was nothing like his usual one. There was something unnerving about it, and it was staring at her from the pages of the newspaper in just the way it had from the lane outside her bedroom window a week ago. Thirty-odd years ago, that picture must have been taken. Thirty years on, and it was almost as if Harold had become the man he had once been made up to portray. But what did it mean?

Heather's immediate inclination was to phone Gerry, but when she tried it was only to be told his mobile was switched off, and as she had no idea where he was, it looked as if she was going to have to sit tight until he phoned her. But there was a good three hours to wait before that, so having checked that all the ground floor doors and windows were locked, she came back up to Tim's den, and switched the video recorder to PLAY.

Jack…

Jack wasn't feeling too clever this morning, having given Moira notice of his 'legacy' last night, before shutting himself away in the spare room with the whisky bottle.

He hadn't intended to put it so crudely – or even to mention it at all, until after he'd been for a blood test. After all, it didn't automatically follow that just because Belinda had had syphilis, he must have it too. But there had been a bit of a commotion outside the theatre last night, and by the time he'd emerged, an area of pavement near the entrance of the multi-storey car park had been cordoned off by the police.

With a sense of foreboding, he'd asked the taxi driver to wait while he tried to find out what was happening, only to have his worst fears confirmed by a world-weary car park attendant, who'd had his early night 'fucked up' by some woman jumping from the third-floor parapet.

After a silent drive home, Jack's distress had been more than Moira could take, and the ensuing row had been brought to a head with the news of Belinda's unwelcome bequest. A genito-urinary disease – that was what they called it – and a genito-urinary clinic was where you went to have it dealt with, rather than an NHS surgery, where details of your treatment were likely to end up on permanent record. Somewhere discreet – that was what was called for in the circumstances – the sort of place that advertised itself on the walls of public toilets.

Moira...

Moira slipped out of the house, and caught the bus across town. She knew there was a code you could dial first, if you didn't want the person you were phoning to know where the call was coming from, but she never trusted herself to get it right, so she inevitably went to a phone box when she needed to make the sort of call she was intending to make this morning. It was inconvenient, but it was only right that someone should tell Belinda's husband that his tart of a wife had had syphilis.

Esther, Alan...

Esther was boarding her train at Victoria when Alan walked into the coach station down the road, and it was with a similar mix of anxiety and determination that each of them was facing the reluctant journey ahead. Both had talked about going home – but only for want of a better word.

Rodney...

Rodney Davis had always been deeply suspicious of therapists and counsellors, and the closest he had ever come to delving into his own psyche was on a self-awareness course he'd been forced to attend last summer, when his company was taken over by an American conglomerate.

Stress management had been part of the curriculum there, but had proved counter-productive in Rodney's case, when his oh-so-reasonable motivator had suggested all sorts of ways of channelling his anger, but none quite as effective as punching him on the nose. He'd nearly lost his job over that, and had been seething about it ever since. But not today. Today it was the furthest thing from his mind.

Heather...

> *"And though I have the gift of prophesy, and understand all mysteries, and all knowledge; and though I have all faith, so that I could remove mountains, and have not charity, I am nothing."*

So says Gabriel Jones, the preacher, in the closing scene of *Shotgunning*, after wreaking terrible vengeance on those sinners amongst his flock who might otherwise have escaped justice. A fall downstairs, a suicide, an accidental overdose – all Gabriel's work – or so the audience is beginning to believe...

> *"Charity suffereth long...is kind...doth not behave itself unseemly..."*

While at his feet, a dumbstruck scandalmonger sees the error of her ways too late.

And Heather sits transfixed.

Downstairs a windowpane shatters on the kitchen floor; but she doesn't hear it.

Esther...

Esther paid off her taxi, and looked up and down the street, which was ominously quiet for a Friday afternoon...or was that just her courage failing her?

The house was quiet too. Of course Dave was probably in the pub, and Esther smiled to herself now, as an unlikely thought occurred to her on the threshold of what promised to be an ugly confrontation.

What if Dave confounded her, by agreeing to go, without so much as a whimper? Unlikely maybe, but it wouldn't be the first time she had spent hours rehearsing an argument that would never take place.

It was while she was searching in her handbag for her front door key, that she noticed something was wrong – an unfamiliar shadow in the corner of one of the frosted window panes that looked out on to the porch – and a moment later she pushed open the door to see Dave's body lying at the bottom of the stairs, while one of Ben's favourite bones hung precariously over the edge of the landing above.

She didn't need to go any nearer to be sure. Her expression barely changed as she stood in the doorway, looking at her husband, her hand still on the key in the lock. She was thinking about Trish, and a recent conversation...

"The defence?" Trish had chuckled. "You haven't bumped him off, have you?"

When she did move it was to turn away, and pull the door closed behind her. Sylvia would know what to do.

Simon…

It hadn't just been Alan's day that had run so close to parallel with Esther's; in fact, if either of them had been in a position to compare notes with Simon, the similarities might have struck them as rather too coincidental.

Esther's train had departed from Victoria this morning, just as Simon was saying goodbye to Polly Hampton. Rehearsals had been cancelled today, so no excuse to delay things any further, and like Esther, Simon had spent the rest of the morning working out what he was going to say when he got home. In the last few minutes he had come to the conclusion that it would serve no useful purpose to challenge Ronnie over his whereabouts on Wednesday night, and had decided instead to tell him the truth – not the evasive truth about how he had tried phoning him several times last night and again this morning, but the real truth, about how he was in love with someone else.

The past few days had done wonders for Simon's self-esteem, despite his having achieved about the lowest score possible in a questionnaire on the subject on Wednesday morning – and it was that that was going to give him the courage to face Ronnie. He paid off his taxi, and looked up and down the avenue, which was ominously quiet…

The house was quiet too. Of course there was no

guarantee that Ronnie was at home, and Simon smiled to himself now, as an unlikely thought occurred to him on the threshold of what promised to be an ugly confrontation.

What if Ronnie confounded him, by agreeing to let him go, without so much as a whimper? Unlikely maybe, but it wouldn't be the first time he had spent hours rehearsing an argument that would never take place.

It was while he was searching in his pocket for his key, that he noticed something was wrong — a light on in the hall in the middle of the day — and a moment later he pushed open the door to find Ronnie on the floor at the bottom of the stairs, where he'd been lying since the early hours of this morning.

There was a look of terror in his eyes, which Simon would come to understand, because although Ronnie was conscious, he had suffered a massive stroke, and he would never volunteer another step or speak another discernible word.

Gerry, Louise, Trish…

Gerry had several phone calls to make this afternoon, the first of which was to Trish and Louise, to confirm that they were still on for tonight. It was Louise who took that one, and unaffected as she was by her years in Hollywood, she was so touched by his offer to send a car to pick them up, she couldn't bring herself to tell him they wouldn't be going. So she told him they would be.

"Sounds like quite a show," she said to Trish afterwards. "The hottest ticket in town, apparently…"

But Trish was unrepentant.

"Word must have got around about the trick with the doughnut," she said, just as the phone started ringing again. "Oh, do me a favour, will you, and put the kettle on while I get that?"

But when she came back, it was more than a cup of tea she was in need of.

"That was Esther's friend Sylvia down in Brighton," she said. "Apparently Dave's fallen downstairs."

Gerry, Heather, Rodney…

Gerry's second call was to Heather – at one o' clock as planned – but when she ran downstairs to answer it, she came face to face with Rodney, last seen dragging Belinda out of the house on Tuesday after the funeral, and fresh from a one-sided telephone conversation with a woman who hadn't given her name.

"Where is he?" he said, pushing Heather back towards the stairs. And he was carrying a knife.

Louise, Trish…

"Platform sixteen," said Louise. "Come on. We've got five minutes."

"Well, I'm not running," said Trish. "If we miss it, we'll just have to get the next one."

They were standing on the concourse at Victoria Station, where they'd been waiting for the platform number to appear on the departure board…and now that it had, the whole world seemed to be on the move. Destination Brighton.

Gerry...

At five past one Gerry tried Heather's number again, but there was still no answer. No point in leaving a message, because he wanted to talk to her personally, and there was a good chance he wouldn't be in a position to pick up if she returned his call. He was due at Effinelli's in half an hour, for one last run-through with Merry's band before tonight's show. He'd have to try again after that.

Rodney, Heather...

Rodney, in the meantime, was trying to make up his mind what to do next, having got nothing out of Heather, apart from a suggestion that Gerry was probably down at his cottage. But he knew that wasn't the case, because he'd drawn a blank there before coming here. So where then?

Of course the answer was that Gerry could be absolutely anywhere, but Rodney had shown his hand now, and that made Heather a liability – particularly if she did know more than she was letting on – so he marched her upstairs at knifepoint, in search of somewhere secure to leave her.

He spotted it through the open door of the main bedroom – a cast iron radiator against the wall opposite – and having ordered her to her knees, he tied her to it, with the flex from a bedside lamp. He didn't notice the photographs on the wall above her head.

Andy, Dan...

Andy and Dan were on days off, so when Sylvia asked them if they'd mind driving to the station to meet a couple of Esther's friends off the train from Victoria, they jumped at the chance to do something for the poor woman, even before it crossed their minds who those friends might be.

"I thought I'd died and gone to heaven," Dan would announce in Legends later. "In fact I wouldn't have been at all surprised if Bette Davis herself had poked her head through the window, and told us all to fasten our seatbelts."

Rodney, Heather...

Rodney was attempting to calm his jangled nerves by doing press-ups on the living room floor, having persuaded himself that he might as well stay put at the Manor House, as Gerry was bound to turn up eventually. He always seemed to be here when Belinda phoned Heather.

Fifty-one, fifty-two, fifty-three, fifty-four...but he was only counting in his head, and it was the sound of his breathing that made him realise how quiet it was in this place. Not at all like the gym.

There was a stereo in the corner, and when he got up to take a closer look, he discovered it was still switched on – with a tape in the deck. So he pressed the button marked PLAY, made a slight adjustment to the volume, and while some poncey Yank spelt out exactly why winter always follows fall, went off to the kitchen to find himself something to eat.

"Have you ever seen a swallow in December...?"

Another of Cordino's favourite songs, apparently, but not one Heather was in a frame of mind to appreciate, and

Rodney obviously hadn't worked out that there were speakers in every room, because he'd adjusted the volume up so he could hear it in the kitchen. It was deafening…and then it was over, and during the blissful silence that followed, Heather managed to convince herself that the tape itself had come to an end. Until it started again…

"You can probably tell by the look on her face…"

But that wasn't Frank Cordino's voice.

Trish, Sylvia, Louise, Esther…

Trish and Sylvia were sitting on a bench overlooking the beach, where Louise was doing her best to wear Ben out with a game of ball, while Esther stood watching them, her mind elsewhere.

"Poor darling," said Sylvia. "She was convinced she was going to be had up for murder, you know. But according to the police, Dave had been there for days, so when I explained that Esther had only just got off the train, the younger one saw exactly where I was coming from, and told us there was no question of her being under suspicion. Now whether that's true or not, I don't know, but it did put Esther's mind at rest, and of course the post mortem will clear up any doubts they do have. Bastard…it was the most considerate thing he ever did, dying while she was away."

Heather, Rodney...

> *"You can probably tell by the look on her face..."*

Heather would have recognised Gerry's voice anywhere.

> *"That the girl never settles for less than the best..."*

It had a catch in it, which made her want to clear her throat.

> *"If only he knew..."*

He was no Frank Cordino.

And clearly Rodney didn't think so either, because before another word could be sung, the sound system fell silent.

Seconds later the telephone in the hall started ringing again, but this time when the answering machine cut in, the caller did leave a message – and once again, there was no mistaking Gerry's voice:

> *"Heather, I don't know where the hell you are, but if you don't pick this up in the next hour, you're going to miss out on one of the best nights of your life. Did you hear the tapes? I hope you liked them, because tonight, you'll be hearing them again – only live. I'm putting on a show at Effinelli's at nine, and I want you at the top table, hurling champagne down your neck like the brave little trouper you are. I'll be sending a car for you at six. Be there!"*

Rodney looked around the room for something to write with…not that he was likely to forget the bits that mattered – Effinelli's…nine o' clock – and then he made his way upstairs.

The forensic evidence would support D I Lawrence's theory that the victim had been tied to the radiator with the flex from an onyx lamp found lying on the bedroom floor; but she'd managed to free herself before her attacker returned. Defensive cuts to the forearms and thighs would indicate that she'd put up a fight; but a stab wound to the heart had proved fatal.

What the evidence would not show was that Heather was standing behind the door when Rodney came into the room; but he spotted her reflection in a photograph hanging on the wall opposite, a split second before she swung the lamp down through the space where his head should have been.

Sylvia, Louise, Trish, Esther…

Seven o' clock now, and having given Andy and Dan some money towards a meal out, Sylvia was doing everything she could to make her guests feel at home. Gin and tonics all round, a shepherd's pie browning in the oven…

"I can't wait," said Louise. "I haven't had shepherd's pie since we were kids."

"Which reminds me," said Trish, turning to Esther. "Have you managed to contact Harold yet?"

"No," said Esther. "Not yet."

"Have you been trying?"

"Not since Wednesday morning, no…"

"Well, I think you should."

"Is this Harold Masters we're talking about?" said Sylvia.

"Yes," said Esther. "I was hoping he'd be at the funeral, actually, but…"

"Maybe he didn't know about it," said Louise.

"Oh, he would have done," said Esther. "Cassie would have told him."

"Who's Cassie?" said Sylvia.

"His neighbour. He hasn't got a television, you see…or a radio – or a phone, come to that – so it's Cassie who keeps him up to date with what's going on in the world. And it's Cassie you have to ring if you want to get in touch with him. But she hasn't been answering…"

"Exactly," said Louise. "And if she's away…"

"Oh…I see what you mean."

"But you haven't tried since Wednesday morning?" said Sylvia.

"No…"

"Well, give us her number, then. I'll go and try it now."

Cassie…

There was a tendency at Calumet to talk about choice – particularly as a way of ending a debate that was going round in circles. For instance…

As the father of the community, Larry was often required to chair policy meetings, where the arguments sometimes got a bit out of hand, and Cassie had always admired the way he stepped in to stop the same points being repeated over and over again.

"Right," he would say. "I think we all know what the

choices are now." And then he'd spell them out, and take a vote. Simple.

Of course things aren't always as clear cut as that, and this evening Cassie is lying on her bed, thinking about something Harold said to her recently, after a particularly frustrating lunch in the community hall. He normally ate alone in his caravan, but a group of American visitors had recognised him when they were being shown around, and invited him to join them.

"They asked me how I came to be here," he said. "And when I told them about my chance meeting with your parents, this Bruce character turned on me with some rubbish about destiny being a matter of choice and not chance. I felt like wringing his smug little neck, but the rest of them just sat round the table nodding their heads, as if it was the most profound thing they'd ever heard."

It wasn't like Harold to let his indignation get the better of him, but when it did, it made Cassie laugh, because she understood what he meant even better than he did; and despite the lonely destiny he'd chosen for himself, it wasn't the sentiment that had infuriated him so much. It was the way it had been expressed.

Cassie wonders what he would have made of her, this man called Bruce. Presumably not even he would have gone so far as to say she'd had any choice but to be born into the community. But he would have said it had been her choice to stay on when her parents left. And he would have said it had been her choice to conduct a thirty-year affair with a married man. And he would have been right. But it was also true that she'd known from the start what a thoughtless bastard Larry could be, so having made her choice then, there really wasn't any point in grousing about it now. Which is why she decided to pull herself together and get up…just as her phone started ringing.

Gerry…

It's ten-fifteen, and at Effinelli's the curtain is about to come down on one of the shortest careers in easy listening history.

"And now…" says Gerry, cue piano…

"And now, the time has come to say goodbye…"

"Well, thank Christ for that!" shouts a joker at a table near the front, and as a gale of drunken laughter rocks the auditorium, Gerry jumps off the stage and kicks his chair from under him, before pushing his way through to the exit, and out into the street.

Cassie…

It was rare for Cassie and Harold to go a day without seeing each other, but it was the best part of a week now since she'd seen him climbing over the fence into the top field…the best part of a week since he'd left her a note saying he was taking himself out of circulation for a while.

But for how long? And what exactly did it mean – out of circulation? He never went anywhere beyond the odd hour or two behind the wheel of that old car of his. He always claimed that that was where he did his best thinking. But six days of it?

Of course, she'd been away herself for four of those days, and she'd spent most of today in bed, so he'd had plenty of time to come and go without her knowing anything about it. And his light had been on when she got back last night, so perhaps his pattern hadn't changed as much as she felt it had.

Anyway, whether or not he was ready to be brought back into circulation, at least now she had the best of reasons for giving it a try.

A woman called Sylvia had phoned earlier asking to speak to him, and when he hadn't been in, she'd left her number, and a request that he should call her back as soon as he could. Esther needed him.

Saturday, 25

Calumet,

April, 1998

Imagine this. On Friday you spent the best part of three hours watching a video of a film that was on television a week ago. It was a Western called Shotgunning, and it starred Harold Masters as Gabriel Jones, an evangelical preacher with paranormal powers.

You've heard a lot about Masters, but nothing to prepare you for the letter you found on your doorstep this morning. It's from him – Harold Masters – and in it he claims to possess the same powers as the man he portrayed in the film. For instance, he says, he can listen in to conversations at any distance.

What do you think? Do you think he's lying? Perhaps you think he's mad? Or do you think instead of a recent conversation of your own, and hope to God he didn't overhear that?

Cassie usually woke up to *The Today Programme* on Radio Four, because she knew that was what Larry did, and it brought him closer to her. But she'd had trouble getting to sleep last night, and then overslept this morning, which is why she didn't hear the news until nine o' clock.

> *"Police are still trying to establish whether there is any link between the discovery of Heather Swallows' body at her home in Wiltshire early this morning, and the stabbing of her brother, television celebrity, Gerry Swallows, outside a club in Islington last night. Mr Swallows was rushed to hospital after an incident outside Effinelli's nightclub at around ten-thirty, but died of his injuries after surgeons failed to revive him."*

By five past nine Cassie was dressed, and out in the clearing, banging on Harold's door again, having drawn a blank last night. But there was still no answer, so this time she broke the golden rule of a community that never locked its doors – and went in uninvited.

No sign of the man himself, but there was a book lying open on his unmade bed, and next to it – an unsealed envelope addressed to Heather in Denby Green. A letter of condolence, presumably…

At nine-fifteen Cassie's phone started ringing, and with Harold's letter still in her hand, she ran over to her caravan to answer it. It was Larry.

"Have you heard the news this morning?" he said.

"I have, yes…"

"So you know about Tim's wife then?"

"Yes…"

"And her brother?"

"Yes…"

"You all right?"

"Yes, of course…just a bit out of breath, that's all. I don't suppose you've seen Harold, have you?"

"That's what I was going to ask you actually, but funnily enough he's walking past my window as we speak."

"Which way's he going?"

"Towards you…do you think I should have a word?"

"No, leave it. I'll tell him…if he doesn't already know."

"Right, thanks. What are you doing in the morning, by the way?"

"Nothing. Why?"

"Jacqui's got a reiki session booked, so I thought I might come over for an hour or so."

"What time?"

"About ten, I think."

"Okay…I'll see you then…"

It took Harold about five minutes to walk from the farmhouse lockups to his caravan – plenty of time for Cassie to make the dash over there, put everything back in place, and get out again – but when he came into the clearing his door was still wide open, and she was sitting on his step with the letter in her hand.

"Cassie…" he said. "Hello…what you doing?"

"Reading," she said. "Listen…

I do possess the same powers as Gabriel Jones…

"Cass…"

"No, don't interrupt. The question and answer session comes at the end. Now…where was I? Oh, yes…

> *Imagine this, the letter starts…*
>
> *I do possess the same powers as Gabriel Jones, and I can listen in to conversations at any distance. I was doing it last Friday evening, lying here in my caravan at Calumet, while a hundred miles away in Denby Green, Tim was thanking Nora Johnson for opening up shop after hours to sell him some aspirin.*
>
> *'I think I must be going mad,' he said, when Nora handed him his change. 'I could have sworn I saw some in the bathroom cabinet this afternoon, but Heather reckons we ran out days ago.'*
>
> *If only I'd followed up on that.*
>
> *But no, because it isn't just the spoken word I can listen in to. I can read minds as well, and one look into Mrs Johnson's eyes was enough to tell me she wasn't really taking in what Tim was saying. She was too keen to get the supper dishes out of the way in time for the film, which was due to start on Channel Four in twenty minutes. It was a Western called Shotgunning, and according to the local paper, it starred Harold Masters as Gabriel Jones, an evangelical preacher with paranormal powers. Imagine that.*

At this point Cassie looked up, expecting some sort of reaction from Harold, but there was none, so she read on:

Strangely enough, my unusual gifts came about as a result of a knock on the head I received during the filming of Shotgunning, an event that coincided with the exact moment of Tim's entrance into the world. I know, because I saw it as clearly as if I'd been present at the birth, instead of several thousand miles away in a mocked-up Western saloon. When I came to, I managed to persuade myself I must have been dreaming – until the telegram arrived – and I was on my way to Tim's christening when I discovered this place.

I never did tell Tim about my powers – in fact the weight of responsibility that came with them was so enormous, I was always a bit cautious about using them at all – but I did suspect I was capable of much more than listening in to conversations and reading minds. So the day after Tim drowned I decided to try something.

I keep a Complete Works of Shakespeare on the shelf above my bed, and I willed it to fall on to a pillow I'd placed underneath it. When it did, I picked it up, and it was open at page 876, in the middle of Act 1V, Scene V11 of Hamlet, Prince of Denmark. Halfway down the left hand column were the lines I was looking for:

*'Too much of water hast thou, poor Ophelia,
And therefore I forbid my tears.'*

Do you know what happened to Ophelia, Heather…when down her weedy trophies and herself fell in the weeping brook?

Yes, of course you do.

Once again, Cassie looked up, and once again Harold returned her look without a word.

> *'Vengeance is mine; I will repay, saith the Lord.'*
>
> *Tim's father quoted that at me once, when I as good as called him a coward for backing away from a fight. I'll never forget it. A couple of yobs had cornered him in an alley, and helped themselves to his wallet. When he told me, I was all for going after them to teach them a lesson. But Oliver had more sense, and I was let off the hook by a line from the Bible.*
>
> *It's a different story now, of course, but then, as Oliver also used to say, God does move in a mysterious way...*

A long pause, and then Cassie put the letter down, and said:

"And it's at this point in the proceedings that we throw the meeting open to a discussion from the floor."

"I didn't send it, Cass," said Harold.

"No," said Cassie. "But you wrote it, didn't you? And now Heather's dead."

"I know...no, Cassie, don't look at me like that. I didn't kill her. I heard it on the radio."

"You haven't got..."

"My car radio."

"Oh...so, you'll have heard about Gerry too, then?"

"Yes."

"And what about Esther's husband?"

"What about him?"

"He's had an accident."

"What…a car accident, do you mean?"

"You really don't know, do you?"

"No, of course not. Why? Did you think I was responsible for that too?"

"I didn't know what to think, Harold. I still don't, to be honest."

"No, well one thing at a time, eh? So…what did happen to Dave?"

"He fell downstairs, apparently. Someone called Sylvia phoned last night wanting to speak to you, but you weren't in, so…"

"So you presumed I'd gone on a killing spree."

"No…I didn't even know about the others then. I just told her you were out, and that I'd get you to call her back when I saw you. You can do it now, if you like. The number's on my desk."

"No answer," said Harold, emerging from Cassie's caravan with a wine bottle in one hand, and two glasses in the other. "I'll try again later. In the meantime, though, I found this in your fridge."

"Well…" said Cassie. "At least that means we're still talking."

"No, it means I'm talking, and you're listening. Questions and answers at the end…right?"

"Right…"

"So…where do I start?"

"With the letter, I would have thought."

"Cassie…"

"Sorry."

"But you're right, actually…that's exactly where to start, and, of course, most of it's complete nonsense. I didn't overhear a conversation between Tim and Nora Johnson; I can't read minds or make books fall off shelves; and I don't see myself as an avenging angel. I just wanted Heather to know I was aware of what she'd done…and I wasn't going to let her get away with it."

"And what had she done?"

"She killed Tim, Cass."

"I've known all along," said Harold, before Cassie could interrupt him with any more questions. "Well, not actually known, but as good as…and then on Thursday night I heard her telling Gerry about it – as if it was something to be proud of – and he just sat there taking it all in, as if it was the sort of thing people did every day. I didn't know what to do."

"Why didn't you go to the police?"

"Because it would have been her word against mine…and I knew who they'd believe. But then she said something about the possibility of having been seen, and I realised she wasn't quite as confident as she'd been pretending to be. So I gave it some thought, and yesterday morning I came up with the idea of writing the letter."

"But you didn't send it?"

"No…it took me till about seven to get it right, and then while I was out in the car – going over it in my head – I remembered something else Heather had told Gerry – about a pair of shoes Tim was wearing when he drowned. So I made up my mind to forget the letter, and phone the police on one of those anonymous hotlines instead. It struck me that if I could persuade them to go round and demand to see the shoes, then perhaps they could get her on forensics – or at least spook her into thinking they were on to her. Anyway, it's all academic now, isn't it?"

"I suppose it is, yes."

"So…what was it you said again? It is at this point in the proceedings…"

"Okay…" said Cassie. "I take it you haven't phoned the police yet?"

"No…"

"So, as far as we know, they don't even suspect Tim was murdered, do they?"

"No."

"And yet you say you've known all along. How?"

"Because I saw Heather behaving suspiciously the night he drowned. She was…"

"But you were here the night he drowned. You had a bad dream, and called out to me. Remember…?"

"Aah…"

"And then on Thursday night you say you overheard Heather telling Gerry all about it?"

"Yes."

"Where was that?"

"At his cottage in Denby Green."

"So where were you at the time…crouching outside his window, on the off chance she might blurt it all out?"

"Not exactly, no…"

"So where then…? And how did you know she'd been watching *Shotgunning*?"

"Sorry, I'm not with you…"

"Yesterday…"

Cassie looked down at the letter, which was still lying open on the step beside her, and read:

"*'On Friday you spent the best part of three hours watching a video of a film that was on television a week ago…'* That's not a question, Harold; it's a statement. So, how did you know?"

And when he didn't answer:

"Harold, we're not by any chance talking astral projection here, are we?"

"I'd never heard of it before I came to this place," said Harold. They were on their second glass of wine now, and well on the way to another bottle. "But I knew there was something funny happening when I had the dream I mentioned in the letter…the one about Tim being born. At least I thought it was a dream, until I discovered it had actually happened.

"Then I moved here, and as much as I loved it, there was so much rubbish talked about that sort of thing, I convinced myself it must have been a coincidence…until a couple of weeks ago, when you lent me Larry's book, and the chapter about out-of-body experiences rang so true, I started thinking there might be something in it after all. So I tried it, and it seems I'm a natural."

"Why didn't you tell me?"

"I was going to…but before I could say anything, I had another dream – about Tim drowning this time…"

"The one you were having when I heard you thrashing about?"

"Yes…only when I visited the scene, that turned out not to have been a dream either. He was floating face down in the pool, fully dressed…but the extraordinary thing was that Heather was in there with him, stripping off his clothes. When she'd finished she took them away and washed them, and then put them back in the changing room to make it look as if he hadn't had them on at all. So…I put two and two together, and I've been keeping an eye on her ever since. That's how I came to hear her telling Gerry about it."

"But you couldn't go to the police, because they'd have wanted to know how you knew what you did?"

"Exactly…and if I'd told them they'd have laughed in my face."

"I would myself, if I didn't know you better. Anyway, bring another bottle when you come back, will you?"

"Why…where am I supposed to be going?"

"To try that Sylvia again…and then we'll have a nice little chat about Esther."

Sunday, 26

Sunday, a.m.

My dear Cassie,

By the time you find this, I'll be on my way to Brighton to propose to the woman I have loved all my life. No leaves falling out of trees, no books falling off shelves – all I can do is hope.
    Wish me luck.

    Love,
        Harold

Esther falls into Harold's arms…credits roll…the end.

At least that's the way Cassie would like it to end. But there's one more question that needs answering first.

It isn't about Dave and his fall downstairs, because according to Sylvia he tripped over a dog's bone. Nor is it connected to Belinda's suicide. Her cry of rape will never be heard. Victor's body hasn't been discovered yet, so it can't be his overdose; and Cassie's never even heard of Ronnie, so it isn't his stroke. On the news this morning it was reported that there'd been some sort of fracas in the club Gerry was in on Friday night – so that probably explains how he came to get stabbed. But what about Heather, the biggest sinner of them all, who was found dead so soon after Harold threatened her with vengeance?

'Do you know what happened to Ophelia, Heather...?'

Is that a coincidence too far?

Cassie turns to the man lying next to her in bed.

"Larry?" she says.

"Sounds ominous," he says.

"What do you mean?" she says. "I only said Larry."

"Go on, then...what?"

"How's your Shakespeare?"

"My Shakespeare? All right, I think...why?"

"Okay...how did Ophelia die?"

"She drowned, didn't she?"

"Did she? She wasn't stabbed, then?"

"No...she definitely drowned."

"Oh, good. I do love a happy ending, don't you?"